sammy KEYES
and the RUNAWAY ELF

sammy KEYES

and the RUNAWAY ELF

WENDELIN VAN DRAANEN

A DELL YEARLING BOOK

Published by Dell Yearling
an imprint of Random House Children's Books
a division of Random House, Inc.
New York

Visit us on the Web! www.randomhouse.com/kids

Educators and librarians, for a variety of teaching tools,
visit us at www.randomhouse.com/teachers

ISBN: 0-375-80255-X

Reprinted by arrangement with Alfred A. Knopf

Printed in the United States of America

May 2000

10 9

In loving memory of my father, Peter Van Draanen, and my brother, Mark. You're in my heart, always.

PROLOGUE

I should have
just said
forget it!

I mean, cruising the streets of Santa Martina on a float with a dozen dogs dressed up like reindeer isn't exactly something I woke up that morning wanting to do. But there I was. Again. In the wrong place at the right time.

And by the time the float turned down Broadway, well, there was no jumping off. Not when I was in charge of a dog worth more than a sleighful of cash.

Of course, if I'd known what was waiting for me just down the street, I'd have jumped, all right.

Jumped and hightailed it *out* of there!

ONE

Grams says Santa Martina is a town just like any other town, but I don't believe it. Sure, it's got a mall downtown and railroad tracks that kind of cut the city into halves, and the two big streets are called Broadway and Main, but after you've lived there a little while you start to realize that Santa Martina is kind of strange. I mean, in the foyer of our city hall there's a statue, and it's not of one of the city's founders or anything historic like a covered wagon or a war hero. No, it's a statue of a group of people down on one knee, hailing a softball.

That's right, a softball.

And even though I'm into softball and I'm really hoping that our team wins the Junior Sluggers' Cup in February, I'm not so far gone that I'd erect a bronze statue like that in City Hall. Mayor Hibbs is. I've heard he dips to one knee as he passes the statue on his way to work, and some people say he even makes the sign of the cross. I've never actually seen him do it, but *someone* put that statue there, and it sure wasn't Father Mayhew.

Aside from the statue there's our calendar. Now, Santa Luisa and other towns around here put out their own calendars too, but theirs are of normal stuff—trees, birds, broken barns—things you expect to see in a calendar.

3

Santa Martina's calendar has mutts. Mangy, misshapen mutts. The weirder looking, the better. The owners dress them up in crazy outfits and take pictures of them at different landmarks around town. Last year, the July dog had on goggles and a scarf, and was parachuting from the roof of the mall. And for October they had a dog chewing on a bone, right outside the cemetery gate. I'm telling you, Santa Martina is not a town like any other town, no matter what Grams says.

Having a cat, I never understood what a big deal the calendar was to dog owners. But then my friend Holly started working for Vera and Meg over at the Pup Parlor and now I know—it's a *huge* deal. Holly says people come in to pick up their dogs and all they talk about is what they're going to do to get chosen for the calendar. Then they go off and launch their pets from rooftops or strap them to motorcycles or get them to scratch up their piano keys, all so they can point to a little brass prize tag and pretend they're a celebrity, riding with their dog in the Christmas parade.

Now I have to admit, the Christmas parade is a great parade—strange, but in a good way. For one thing, it's at night. Everyone puts Christmas lights on their float—big ones, tiny ones, icicle ones—and when all those lights come riding down Broadway, well, it *feels* like Christmas.

People go all out, too, and I don't think it's because the first-place float gets a candy cane the size and shape of a softball bat. I think it's because everybody wants to outdo the guy who outdid them the year before. There are flatbed trucks with forests of pine trees, and carolers standing on snow that's been hauled down from the mountains. There are floats on wagons with lots of hay and people and real animals making up Nativity scenes. There are even motorcycle floats. Last year the Harley club entered, and when Grams saw them growling down the street on their hogs, decked out as rebel Santas, she called them "Biker Santas from You-Know-Where" and plugged her ears.

So it's a fun parade to watch, but Marissa's actually been *in* it a couple of times, and she says that's boring. You have to wait forever in line, and then it's stop-and-go, stop-and-go down Broadway for almost two hours. On top of that, you don't actually get to *see* the parade.

So I've always been happy to sit on the curb, waving and clapping for wagons of sheep and "Biker Santas from You-Know-Where." And this year I was planning to meet Grams at our usual spot, right after I got done helping Holly and Vera get the Canine Calendar float ready. The problem was, I couldn't find the float. I ran down Wesler Street, where everyone lines up before the parade, but I couldn't remember if their float was number sixty-eight or eighty-six.

When I got to the sixties, I stopped and asked a lady dressed up like the Virgin Mary, "Have you seen the Canine Calendar float?"

She blinked at me and asked, "What?"

"You know, the float with all the dogs?"

Mary shook her head and went back to arranging straw around Baby Jesus. "You got me."

So I figured it had to be eighty-six. I kept on running,

past the firemen's float, past a couple of Santa's workshop floats and a bunch of horses munching on hay through the slats of a wagon. Finally I stopped and asked a clarinet player in the Santa Martina High School marching band, "Have you seen the Canine Calendar float?"

She straightened her hat. "The what?"

"You know—the float with all the dogs?"

She shook her head. "What number is it?"

"Eighty-six, I think."

"It would have to be back that way. We're one-oh-two."

So I turned around and ran back the way I'd come. And I'm running along, dodging Santas and elves and horses and wagons, when all of a sudden I hear, "Sammy! Over here!"

Well, sure enough, it's Holly, calling me from down a side street. I run over, and she says, "You're not going to believe what a mess things are!"

"What's wrong?"

"The bracket to hold up the wreath snapped, they can't get the lights to work, and Mr. Petersen keeps yelling at everybody. He's making the dogs so nervous that they're snapping at each other and they won't wear their antlers." She picked up Vera's little dog and said, "And Hero keeps trying to lift his leg on Lucy!"

I tried not to laugh. I mean, Lucy's like a cross between a Chihuahua and a toy poodle, and I couldn't imagine another dog *bothering* to pee on her. But it was easy to see that Holly was upset, so I just asked, "Who's Hero?"

"That wanna-be dalmatian over there."

I looked at the float and knew right away which dog she meant. His body was spotted like a dalmatian, but he had the long droopy ears and face of a basset hound. And on the very tip of his tail was a tuft of long red hair—like his great-great-granddaddy had been an Irish setter and was fighting to be remembered.

I laughed. "That is one strange-looking dog."

"You can say that again."

"So who's Mr. Petersen?"

She rolled her eyes. "The guy who puts together the calendar." She pointed at a man with oily hair wearing a black tuxedo with tails. "He is such a jerk."

Now I couldn't help it—I laughed. "He looks like a giant stinkbug!"

Holly's eyes popped open. "He…he does…!"

Just then Mr. Petersen yelled, "And where the devil is Marique? I should never have let that prima donna in the calendar! Someone get on the phone and find out where that stupid dog is. If she's a no-show, I'm ripping her off the cover!"

A lady with some kind of cross-eyed terrier muttered, "Good idea anyway, if you ask me," which made the people around her nudge each other and chuckle.

One of the men working on the float called, "If she's a no-show, we don't need this wreath, Royce!"

"Just fix the wreath!"

I rolled my eyes at Holly and whispered, "Tell me again why you were so excited about Lucy being on the float?"

She laughed. "I don't remember right now."

So we're all kind of keeping our distance from Mr. Petersen, when a girl in jeans and a red jacket comes up carrying a dog under her arm like a furry football. She says, "Mr. Petersen?"

"Yeah, what?"

"I'm Tina Landvogt." She holds out the dog and says, "My mother's in the hospital with a broken leg, but she still wants Marique in the parade."

Mr. Petersen looks around for a minute, not taking the dog. "So are you gonna show her?"

Tina shakes her head. "I can't. I've got to videotape the parade for my mother." She shoves the dog into his arms and says, "Besides, she doesn't want me to do it. She wants Vera to."

So there he is, the world's biggest stinkbug, holding this miniature lion like it's a baby with a dirty diaper. He blinks around at us, then notices Vera. "You! Here! You're in charge of this."

Vera says very carefully, "I never said I would show Lilia's dog. Besides, I have Lucy to show."

"I thought your girl was showing your dog."

"Yes, but I'm—"

"Then you can deal with this thing."

He tried to give her the dog, but Vera wouldn't take it. "No, Royce. I'm photographing the parade."

"This is more important than some silly snapshots!"

Now Vera isn't big, but she could wrestle Mr. Petersen into a flea-dipping tank quicker than you or I could spell his name. And standing there getting yelled at by the Big Bug, you could tell she was thinking that's exactly what the man needed. She crossed her arms and said, "No, sir. I made arrangements for my dog. You find someone else."

But in the middle of saying that, she looks around and notices me. She waits a minute, then motions me over and whispers, "Sammy, why don't you show her?"

"Me?"

"Sure. She's a good dog, and really, the float isn't much without her."

"Why's that?"

She points over to the wreath that they've finally got to stand up. "Marique's the one that jumps through the hoop."

"What about Meg? I could run and get her—"

"No, she's home with the flu, sicker than a dog. I feel bad even being away from her."

Mr. Petersen sees us whispering and shouts, "You! What about you?"

"Me?" I blink at him a bunch and say, "I don't know anything about showing a dog!"

Holly whispers, "C'mon! It'll be fun. I'll help you."

"Why don't *I* take the pictures and *Vera* can show the dog?"

Vera shakes her head and says, "I don't think you'll be able to handle the camera. It's got a telephoto and a zoom. There's no autofocus and the meters are hard to read until you know what you're looking for. I don't think I can teach you in five minutes."

It did look more like a cannon than a camera, so I said, "Okay, okay! I'll show the dog."

I had *no* idea what I was getting myself into.

TWO

By the time Mr. Petersen maneuvered our float forward to join the rest of the parade, Hero had run out of ammunition and the other dogs had settled down a bit. Some of them were still trying to shake their antlers loose, but pretty much they just sat next to their owners, looking ridiculous.

And I was concentrating so hard on Marique jumping back and forth through the wreath that I wasn't really paying attention to anything else. Not until Holly called, "Hey, Sammy! Isn't that your favorite cop?"

Now I haven't known Holly all that long, and it's kind of a long story, but she understands better than anyone else I know what it's like to avoid the police. And it's not like I'm a lawbreaker or anything. I mean, I don't shoplift or break into houses—nothing like that. It's just that I'm living with my grams at the Senior Highrise, and over there, kids are like rats; if someone thinks there's one in the building, they're going to set traps until it's caught.

And there's no one who would like to snap my tail more than Officer Borsch. Well, except maybe my neighbor Mrs. Graybill.

And I'd recognize Officer Borsch anywhere. Even somewhere you'd never expect to see him. Like in a

Christmas parade. On a horse. And since I'd never seen him ride anything but a squad car before, to me he looked pretty uncomfortable, swaying back and forth up there in the saddle. And I know that horses are supposed to be pack animals, but let me tell you, the *horse* looked pretty uncomfortable, too. Like he'd never had to carry a load quite like Officer Borsch before and was having trouble getting him balanced.

I called back to Holly, "I don't believe it!"

She laughed. "Don't worry about it. He's not going to notice you."

I watched him for a minute, but then I got back to concentrating on Marique. And after we turned onto Broadway I'd actually forgotten about Officer Borsch and was starting to have fun. The street was packed with people, and when we drove by they clapped and whistled and shook their jingle-bell sticks so hard that you'd have thought Marique was jumping through fire instead of a hoop of pine branches. Some of them even called out, "Go, Marique, go!" like she was a real celebrity.

And when we got to the place I was supposed to meet up with Grams, sure enough, there she was, with Hudson, looking everywhere but at the parade, worried. I hollered, "Hey, Grams! Hudson! Up here!" and waved real big.

Hudson grabbed Grams' arm and pointed. And Grams' face went from worried, clear through shocked, all the way to relieved in about two seconds. She waved back and laughed, and when Marique jumped through the wreath, she had the biggest smile in the crowd.

So we were putting along and everything was going fine,

and then we hit Cook Street. Cook is where the judging starts. It's also where the biggest crowds gather. There's a mall parking lot on one side and a big church parking lot on the other, so there's lots of room for people to stand.

If you've ever been in a parade you know: sometimes it's real noisy—people are clapping and cheering and there's music blaring over loudspeakers and the marching band is playing—and sometimes it's quiet. Completely quiet. Like in class, when everyone's talking all at once and then all of a sudden *nobody's* talking.

So there we were, at the corner of Broadway and Cook, waiting, when suddenly there's this wave of quiet. And that's when I notice these three people dressed up like the Three Kings stepping off the curb and into the street. They're wearing robes with the hoods up, and they're kind of looking down so you can't see their faces.

At first I thought they were just late joining a float, but then I notice that they're not carrying gold, frankincense, or myrrh—they've got cats. Scared, panicked cats.

And while my brain's trying to absorb the fact that the Three Kings are bearing their gifts straight toward our float, through the quiet I hear, "Maaaariiique! Maaaar-iiique!"

Well, Marique goes charging through the hoop and straight off the float. And while I'm calling, "Marique! Marique, come back!" she flies across the street, through the crowd, and into the darkness.

I swung my legs over the edge of the float, but we were moving forward and the bed of the truck was quite a ways up, so I couldn't exactly jump. Mr. Petersen yells out his window, "What are you doing? Get back on!" but does he slow down? Not at all. Finally I just flip around, hang over, and let go, and as I'm getting my balance, I see the Three Kings, right at our float. I yell, "Hold on to your dogs!" but it's too late—cats are already sailing through the air.

Reindeer antlers went flying everywhere. Hero charged across the float and knocked down the wreath, then a bull-dog with a mane like a chow leapt off into the street, and before you know it everyone was scrambling off the float to chase their dogs.

They went in every direction, but the furry bulldog decided to take a shortcut—straight under Officer Borsch's horse. Well, that spooked the horse so badly that he neighed and pulled a giant horsy wheelie, and even though Officer Borsch held on like a koala to a tree, it wasn't long before he was sitting on asphalt.

By the time everyone got their jaws back in socket, the Kings were gone. I wanted to track them down and deliver a gift of my own, but I had to find Marique. So I ran through the crowd calling, "Marique! Marique! Here, girl!" but I didn't see her anywhere. I asked a lady, "Did a little dog run through here?"

She laughed, "Which one?"

"She's furry—kind of orange. The one that was jumping through the wreath…?"

A woman standing next to her said, "The Pom? She went straight through there," and pointed across the mall lawn. "Cute dog!"

I ran across the lawn and looked everywhere, but no Marique. Finally I asked a man in the parking lot, "Has a dog come through here? Little. Furry. Orange...?"

He shook his head. "Ain't seen one."

I spent the next two hours chasing around the mall, asking people if they'd seen Marique—nobody had. I called Grams and told her about the feline fiasco, then started searching farther into the neighborhoods around the mall. But the later it got, the fewer people I ran into, and nobody had seen Marique.

I was about to give up and go home when I passed by the library and noticed someone sitting on the root of a giant fig tree in the library lawn.

I decided to go ask if they'd seen Marique, but the closer I got the slower I walked, until finally I just stopped and stared. And I could feel my heart start to beat a little funny because I realized that it wasn't a person sitting on the root of that tree—it was an elf. A real live elf.

I was afraid to get any closer. I was afraid somehow it would disappear. So I just stood there in the dark watching the elf kind of glow in the moonlight.

Finally I moved in, little by little, and the elf didn't disappear. She kept right on sitting there, looking up at the moon. When I got close enough I realized that she was just a little girl in an elf costume, but I was still having trouble shaking off the feeling that I'd found a real live elf. Finally I whispered, "Hi."

She just kept staring.

"Hi...um...I was wondering..." I said, but all of a sudden I wasn't really wondering about Marique—I was wondering about *her*. I sat down one root over. "What are you doing?"

She looked at me for a second, then went back to staring at the moon. "Nothing."

I looked at the moon, too. "Well, what are you thinking?"

For a long time she didn't say a word. She just stared up at the sky. Finally she let out a little sigh and whispered, "I wonder what it's like."

I waited a minute. "What what's like?"

"To be up there."

"On the moon?"

She shrugged. "Just up there."

I watched her, watching the moon. Finally I asked, "Were you in the parade?"

She kicked the grass with her little elf boot and muttered, "Stupid parade."

"What happened?"

She looked at me like I ate toads. "Nothing. It's just stupid."

All of a sudden I couldn't help laughing. "Yeah. I know what you mean."

She eyed my sweatshirt and high-tops. "*You* were in the parade? As what?"

"I was on the Canine Calendar float."

Her eyes popped open. "The one that went berserk?"

I laughed and said, "That would be the one. And I've been looking all night for the dog I was taking care of."

"Which one was it?"

I shrugged. "Little orange fuzzy thing. Looks like a tiny lion."

"The Pomeranian? The one on the cover?"

I looked at her and asked, "How'd you know that?"

"Our calendar came in the mail today." She squinted a little. "Do you like Pomeranians?"

I laughed. "I didn't even know she was a Pomeranian! I just got talked into showing her because the lady who owns her is stuck in the hospital with a broken leg."

She seemed relieved. "So you'd rather have a sheep-dog?"

"A *sheep*dog?"

She rolled her eyes and grumbled, "You sound just like my mom."

Now I was about to ask her where her mom was, anyway, when both of us noticed a police car cruising by the library. And when it passed by a streetlight, we both moaned, "Oh no, not him!"

I blinked at her and asked, "You know Officer Borsch?"

She jumped to her little elf feet. "How do *you* know him?"

I followed her across the lawn, but we hadn't made it more than ten steps when a floodlight about blinded us.

I turned away from the light, and then Ol' Borsch-head's voice blares, "Elyssa, stop!"

She stands there with her arms crossed and a great big elf-pout on her face. "I can go home by myself! Leave me alone!" She nods in my direction and calls, "Besides, she's taking me home."

"Oh?" He starts moving in on us, asking, "And who is 'she'?"

I turn to face him and call, "It's me, Officer Borsch. Sammy."

Well, that stops him dead in his tracks. And you can tell that what he really wants to do is sit down and cry. But instead he takes a deep breath, motions back at the squad car to cut the lights, and then there we are, in the moonlight, in the middle of the library lawn, staring at each other.

Finally Officer Borsch sighs and says, "So, Elyssa. You're friends with Samantha. Why am I not surprised."

All of a sudden there's a little elf hand in mine. "Yeah," she says, "and I'm not going anywhere without her."

Officer Borsch nods a bit, then eyes me and says, "Is *she* the reason you're always running off, Elyssa?"

Now, it would really make Officer Borsch's holiday season if he could pin something on me—anything. But Elyssa digs in and says, "I'm not going home without her."

He shakes his head and says, "Suit yourself," then motions toward the car. "Let's go."

So off we go. And the minute he's got us tucked in the backseat, Elyssa scoots right over to the door and stares out the window at the moon. After we get going, she gropes around behind her until she's holding my hand. Her fingers are cold and little, and I wonder—what is she looking at out there?

And what is she thinking, this little runaway elf?

THREE

Elyssa's mom didn't look anything like an elf. As a matter of fact, she was kind of tall. She came charging through the front door when we pulled up, crying, "Oh, baby, where have you *been?*"

Elyssa didn't say a word. She hugged her mom back, but the whole time she wouldn't let go of my hand. Finally the Elf Mom looks at Officer Borsch and says, "Where did you find her, Gil?"

"Near the library."

"The *library?*" She turns to Elyssa and whispers, "What were you doing at the library?"

Elyssa shrugs, then gives her mom a smile and asks, "Can she stay?"

"Can she...?" The Mom blinks at me a minute, then turns to Officer Borsch for help.

Officer Borsch clears his throat like he's sorry to have to break the bad news to her. "This is Samantha Keyes. I found them together outside the library."

She looks me up and down. "What were you doing with my daughter?"

Now, I didn't really like the way she was saying it—like I'd been teaching her little elf to play poker or something.

But I took a deep breath and said, "I was looking for a dog that ran away from me, and I found her instead."

She looked at me like she didn't quite believe her ears. "You were looking for a dog and you found my daughter?"

I shrugged and nodded, and then all of a sudden Elyssa lets go of my hand and runs into the house. She comes back a minute later with the Canine Calendar and shows her mom the cover. "This one."

Well, there's Marique, all right, looking like a snotty little lion on a sheepskin rug with a cigarette holder in one paw and a champagne glass with *Santa Martina Valley, Home of the Best* etched across it in the other.

Elyssa's mom says, "That's *your* dog?"

I'm about to say, "No, ma'am!" and explain about Mrs. Landvogt, when I notice Officer Borsch standing there, getting redder and redder. He spits out, "*You* were on that float? No wonder!"

I put both hands up. "Now wait a minute...! I didn't have anything to do with it!"

Elyssa's mom says, "Gil, don't. Remember your blood pressure. Besides, it wasn't that bad."

He looks at her a minute and then chokes out, "You saw it, too?"

She shrugs and says, "It was only on for a second."

"On? Oh, Janet, no! Not on TV!"

"Only for a second, Gil, now take it easy."

"Take it *easy*? You know what it's like—the guys are going to torture me with this! I'll be the laughingstock at briefing tomorrow."

"No you won't. Anyone could see that it wasn't your fault."

"No, I *know*," he says, and looks straight at me. Now I'm about to say it wasn't *my* fault either, but before I can, he says, "I gotta get back. Janet, you call me if you need anything, and Elyssa, mind your mother! This running away bit has got to stop."

Elyssa just sticks her tongue out at him.

Elyssa's mom gives her a scolding look, then says, "Thanks again, Gil."

So I'm standing there holding my breath, hoping that Officer Borsch has forgotten about me, when he gets to the curb and calls, "Get in, Samantha, I'm taking you home."

Oh man! What am I supposed to do now? See, Officer Borsch thinks I live clear out on East Jasmine. It's kind of a long story, but as far as he knows, I live with my best friend, Marissa. And since East Jasmine is *miles* away from the Senior Highrise, if I let Officer Borsch take me there I'm going to have to spend the rest of the night walking back.

So when Elyssa grabs my hand and says, "No! I want her to stay!" I start breathing again and call, "Thanks anyway, but I think I'll stay here awhile."

He shrugs, then zooms off. And when I turn around, there's Elyssa's mom, checking me out like I have a third eye somewhere. Finally she says, "Why don't you come in for a minute?"

Now really, I don't want to. I want to get home to Grams and maybe call Holly and Vera to see if they know anything about Marique. But Elyssa tugs me up the steps, and before you know it I'm in their house with the Elf welded to me on one side and the Elf Mom staring at me from the other.

The Mom says, "Elyssa, why don't you bring your new friend a soda."

Elyssa looks up at me like that's a great idea. "What do you want?"

The Elf Mom doesn't take her eyes off me. "Anything, Elyssa. Get her a black cherry...anything."

Elyssa runs off, and all of a sudden her mom squints at me and says, "Hudson's! That's where I've seen you before. Down the street at Hudson Graham's. Are you a relative of his?"

I dig at the carpet with my high-top and say, "No, just a friend." And it's true—he may be seventy-two and have a few marbles on the loose when it comes to cowboy boots, but he's my friend. My good friend.

"Hmm," she says. "Hmm." Then she shakes her head "Okay, well anyhow, tell me what you were doing with Elyssa."

"What was I *doing* with her? Nothing. I saw her under the tree, and I went up to ask her if she'd seen the dog."

Her face softened up a bit as she plopped into an easy chair. "You didn't talk about *any*thing?"

"Not really—she was just looking at the moon."

She put her face in her hands and groaned, "The moon again...what am I going to *do* with that child?"

Elyssa comes bouncing back and hands me a can of soda. "Here you go!" she says, then sips from a glass, full almost to the brim. "I took a little, okay?"

I shake what's left in the can and can't help but laugh. "Sure," I say. "Have all you want."

The Mom doesn't even notice. She says, "Elyssa, what were you doing tonight?"

"Just watching, Mom." Elyssa smiles at me and says, "It's good, huh?"

I sip a lot of air and say, "Uh-huh."

Elyssa gives her mom a hopeful look. "Can Sammy stay over?"

"Stay over?" I put the soda can down. "I've got to get home! My...um...mom is going to be real worried if I don't show up soon."

Elyssa's mother jumps up and says, "See, Elyssa! That's what you're supposed to do. You're supposed to come home so your mom doesn't worry."

Elyssa looks at me, then looks down at her little elf boots. She doesn't tell her mom she's sorry or promise never to do it again. What she does is peek up at me and say, "Can you come back tomorrow?"

Well, what am I supposed to do? I shrug and say, "I guess so. If it's okay with your mom."

The Elf Mom sighs, "If that's what she wants, it's fine with me."

I got out of there as fast as I could, and the minute I hit the sidewalk, I hung a left and went two doors down. To Hudson's.

The lights were out, and for a minute I thought he'd gone to bed, but just as I'm about to turn around I hear, "Sammy! What brings you here at this hour?"

So I went through the gate, and sure enough, there's

Hudson in the dark on the porch, watching the moon. I sit down next to him without a word.

He pulls on one of his bushy white eyebrows and says, "I saw the news. There wasn't much left of that float of yours when it passed by the judges." He gives me a funny little smile. "Is that what's brought you here?"

So I sigh and tell him. All about Stinkbug Petersen and his stupid antlers, and about getting talked into taking care of Marique. And when I get to the part about the Three Kings and the cats he says, "Ahhh...that would explain the condition of the float."

"Yeah..."

He studies me a second, then says, "I know that look. What's cooking up there?"

"I'm not sure..."

"But...?"

"But the more I think about it, the more I'm sure that Heather Acosta was one of those Kings."

He went back to tugging on an eyebrow. "So the demon resurfaces."

I laughed, and said, "Well, it's not like I've got proof or anything, and I don't really know how she could've found out so fast that I was going to be on the float—it just seems like something she would do." I let out a sigh and looked up at the moon. "The trouble is, I can't blame losing Marique on Heather—if it *was* Heather. Marique jumped off the float *before* it got bombed with cats."

"Oh?"

"It was really weird. I heard someone call, 'Maaaariiique! Maaaariiique!' and then all of a sudden she charged right off the float."

"Why's that so strange?"

"Because a lot of people called her name. We'd be driving by and someone would call, 'Go, Marique, go!' or whistle and clap and call her name. She ignored all of them. Then all of a sudden she hears her name and *zoom!* off she goes."

"Hmmm," he says. "Have you called Mrs. Landvogt? Maybe the dog's been returned to her."

"You think so?"

"It's worth a try."

So I went inside and dug through the phone book. I found a Landsford, a Landstad, two Landwers, but no Landvogt.

Hudson shrugged. "Why don't you give Vera a call? She'll probably have her number."

It was pretty late, but I decided to do it anyway.

Holly answered, "Hello?"

"It's Sammy."

"Oh, Sammy! Oh, thank God. Have you got Marique? Mrs. Landvogt's called here twenty times wanting to know about her dog."

"Rats."

"What? You *haven't* got her?"

"No. I've been looking for her all night."

"Ho-boy." She was quiet for a minute, then whispered, "Vera's a nervous wreck. Mrs. Landvogt's threatening to get her business license revoked."

"*What?*"

"Yeah. She's blaming it all on Vera."

"It's not Vera's fault!"

Holly laughed. "Try to tell Mrs. Landvogt that!"

"What a mess." I sat there a minute, thinking. Finally I said, "Well, I've looked everywhere for her and I don't know what else to do. If you hear anything, call me at home, okay?"

I got off the phone, and as I'm heading out the door I ask Hudson, "Do you know that little girl who lives down the street? Elyssa?"

"Keltner? Sure. She comes over here once in a while." He kicked his boots up on the porch railing and grinned. "Usually right after I've baked a chocolate cake."

"What do you know about her?"

"She's a cute little thing...wants a sheepdog...doesn't like her brothers too much. They're twins, and I guess they don't let her tag along very often." He dusted off a boot. "The mother seems nice—I don't know about the father, I haven't met him. They've only lived there about six months." He looked me over. "Why do you ask?"

"Just wondering."

"Oh, come on, Sammy. You don't 'just wonder' about things. Out with it!"

So I sat down next to him and said, "I guess she runs away a lot."

"Oh?"

"Yeah, and when I was out looking for Marique I found her instead, and now she's acting like I'm her best friend."

He eyed me. "So be her best friend."

"She's only like seven or eight years old!"

He looks at me like, So? and all of a sudden I realize that the difference between thirteen and seven is a lot less than the difference between thirteen and seventy-two. And thinking about that made me feel uncomfortable. Very uncomfortable.

I stood up and said, "I've...I've got to get home. Grams is probably starting to get worried."

He just smiled at me and said, "Tell her I say hi."

The whole way home it bothered me. I mean, was my hanging around Hudson like the Elf wanting to hang around me? And if it was, why in the world did he let me do it?

I was on autopilot, going up the fire-escape stairs, sneaking down the hall, thinking about Hudson and Elyssa, when all of a sudden there's my grandmother, in the hallway with a fireman. Then I notice that Mrs. Graybill's door isn't cracked open a few inches like it usually is so she can spy on me—it's wide open. I run up to Grams and whisper, "What happened? Did she start a fire?"

Grams says, "No. Apparently she fell."

Just then two paramedics roll out a stretcher, and on it is Mrs. Graybill. I take one look at her and whisper, "Is she dead?" because even though Mrs. Graybill usually looks kind of pale behind her matted hair and crooked lipstick, her eyes were closed and she looked as white as the sheets.

Well, she must've heard my voice, because one of her eyes opens up a crack and her lips move a bit, like she's trying to get out her last words—There she is! Catch her!

One of the paramedics whispers, "She's got a broken arm and she's pretty bruised up, but she's going to be fine."

Grams steps forward and says, "Don't you worry, Daisy. You're going to be all right."

Mrs. Graybill just closes her eye and shakes her head.

So off they go to the elevator, and when they're out of sight, Grams says, "This has been some night."

"You can say that again."

"You didn't find the dog?"

"Nope."

Grams opens our door and says, "Marissa called. She wants you to call her back, no matter what time it is."

So I went into the kitchen and punched in Marissa's number, and before it had even rung once, Marissa snatched it up with, "Sammy?"

"Yeah."

"God, this is so weird. This is so weird."

"What?"

"I got this call from our neighbor, Mrs. Landvogt..."

"Wait a minute! Mrs. Landvogt is your *neighbor*?"

"Yeah, she lives kitty-corner, across the street."

Now on East Jasmine, kitty-corner across the street is about the same as two blocks down. And since Marissa's never talked about any of her neighbors, I figured they didn't really have block parties out there on East Jasmine, if you know what I mean.

"Do you *know* her?"

"No. My mom's met her, but I don't really know anything about her."

"But she called you? Not your mom, you?"

Now I could just see Marissa, pacing back and forth in her room, doing the McKenze dance. "That's what's so weird. She calls, and get this—she says, 'Have Samantha report to my house tomorrow at nine A.M. I want no excuses—have her here.'"

"Wait a minute...I thought she was in the hospital!"

Marissa laughed. "Well, she's home now."

"How did she know we were friends?"

"I don't know! And I asked her, 'Samantha *Keyes?*' but all she said was, 'Have her here at nine!' and then she hung up."

I let what she'd said soak in. "Maybe Vera told her."

"Maybe. I don't know. All I know is that we'd better be over there at nine tomorrow morning."

"We?"

"Sure, I'll go with you."

I laughed and said, "Okay. I'll be at your house at quarter of."

I got off the phone telling myself that none of this was my fault—that really, all I owed her was maybe an apology. But inside I had the awful feeling that an apology was not going to cut it.

Not with Mrs. Landvogt.

FOUR

I was expecting big. I mean, Marissa could have a slumber party for the whole seventh grade at her house and her mom might not even notice. That's East Jasmine for you. But when we rang the doorbell at Mrs. Landvogt's house, even Marissa's eyes were bugged out.

And you'd better believe if *she* felt a little out of place standing on a marble porch the size of Grams' living room, I felt like a beggar at the palace gate. I kept looking over my shoulder, kind of wondering if someone was going to shoot me for trespassing.

Marissa tugged on my arm and whispered, "Get a load of the mail slot!"

At first I couldn't believe it. "Is that *gold*?"

She nodded, then pointed to the knocker. It was a gold bull's head with a giant ring through the nose.

I whispered, "That is so ugly!"

"Shhh!" She pushed the doorbell again and we could hear it ringing inside. "Maybe she forgot."

I rolled my eyes and said, "Right."

Now, you'd expect at a place like the Landvogt mansion that a guy in a suit and bow tie would answer the door with his nose in the air, but instead it was Tina Landvogt. And even though you could see up her nose pretty good, she wasn't wearing any bow tie. Just jeans and boots and an oversized T-shirt.

She smiled at Marissa. "Sammy?"

Marissa shook her head and pointed to me. "She's Sammy."

Tina hitched her thumb behind her. "Mother's upstairs." We stepped inside, and as she closed the door I could hear a faint *bo-beep* sound like a chime hiccuping. Tina pulled back the entryway curtain and switched on the Christmas-tree lights. "And I'm afraid she's in a pretty foul mood."

As we followed her through the foyer, Marissa grabbed my arm and whispered, "Check out that chandelier!"

It looked more like a crystal carousel than a light fixture. We walked under it like we were watching a comet cross the sky, and when we turned the corner there were two more, sparkling away in the dining room.

And we were so busy gawking that we didn't even notice Tina stop and open the elevator door. "C'mon, girls, all aboard."

Marissa practically choked. "An *elevator*?"

We stepped inside, and while we were inspecting the baby chandelier hanging from its ceiling, Tina pushed a button and said, "It's come in pretty handy for getting Mother up and down."

Since she was smiling, I decided to ask, "How'd she break her leg, anyway?"

"Tripping over that stupid dog."

"Marique?"

She laughed. "The one and only." The elevator clanked

to a stop, and as Tina opened the gate, we heard the doorbell ring. She scowled and muttered, "This playing doormaid stuff is getting old in a hurry." She pointed us to a room with its double doors wide open. "Mother knows you're here. Just go in." She headed back to the elevator and whispered, "Good luck."

Now, I have to admit that my heart was popping around pretty good, but I kept telling myself that there was really nothing she could do to me. She could rant and rave and call me names, but when that was over, what could she do? Make me clean her chandeliers?

So we inched over to the doorway of this enormous bedroom, and what we saw was white. White curtains, white furniture, white carpet, even the TV was white. And there, propped up in the middle of a huge puffy white bed, was Mrs. Landvogt. Only she wasn't white, she was green. Emerald green. She had on a shiny green night-gown and a matching robe. Her hair was all wrapped up in this green turban contraption, and her three-inch nails looked like she'd gone down to the body shop and dipped them in sports-car paint.

Her leg was propped up on a pillow with the cast sticking out past the bottom of her robe, and she was punching buttons on a remote control. And while we're standing there, gawking from behind her, she says without looking over, "You'll get in here if you know what's good for you."

We shuffle in, and she points to the TV, saying, "Look at that—there she goes. Try to tell me you didn't just let her get away."

That's when it hit me that what she's watching is a

videotape of the parade, and she's wearing out the thirty seconds where Marique jumps off the float.

"See? You're just standing there!" She pauses the video, then advances it frame by frame. Sure enough, there I am, standing in the background like a bug-eyed totem pole.

She snaps, "Why didn't you stop her?"

"I'm...I'm sorry, Mrs. Landvogt. I got off the float as fast as I could!"

She lets the tape go regular speed, and right after the dogs abandon the float, the TV goes fuzzy with static. She presses the rewind button. "You call this fast?"

"If you play it at regular speed—"

"Quiet!"

Marissa and I jump back like we've been snapped at by a crocodile and stand there watching Marique jump off the float again, frame by frame.

Mrs. Landvogt turns to me and hisses, "And don't try to blame it on the cats!"

"I'm not, ma'am, but they did—"

"Stop with the excuses!"

"But—"

"Stop!"

We stare at each other a minute, and when she's sure I'm not going to say another word, she buffs the nail of a thumb and says, "So..."

But then there's a knock on the door. We all turn around and look, and there, standing on the threshold with a piece of folded paper in her hand, is Tina.

Mrs. Landvogt snaps, "Didn't I make it clear that I didn't want to be interrupted?"

"Yes, but I thought you'd want to see this."

She gives Tina an annoyed look, then says, "What is it?"

Tina steps into the room and hands her the paper. "It was dropped through the mail slot. I ran outside, but I didn't see anybody. I'm sorry."

Mrs. Landvogt takes the paper and says, "This is a..." she flips it open, "a *ransom* note?"

Tina stands there like a whipped puppy, nodding.

Marissa and I scoot in a little closer. On the outside of the note there are magazine letters pasted together spelling LILIA LANDVOGT. And inside is: YOU WANT YOUR DOG? I WANT $50,000. CALL THE COPS AND I'LL CUT HER THROAT.

All of a sudden Mrs. Landvogt turns the color of her decor. "No...!" After a minute she waves a green claw through the air and cries, "Fifty thousand dollars! Are they *insane*? No dog is worth fifty thousand dollars!" She slaps the note with the back of her hand. "What kind of monster would steal my baby?"

Tina whispers, "You want me to call the police?"

"No!"

"You're not going to *pay* it, are you?"

"Not if I can help it." She buffs her thumbnail a minute, thinking. Finally she says, "I need a few minutes with Samantha. Alone."

Tina whispers, "Let's go" to Marissa, and they scurry out, closing the doors behind them.

So there I am in this big white room, alone with this woman who's looking more and more like a crocodile every second. She rearranges her pillows a bit and then smiles at me. "So."

Now I'm not sure if she's planning to eat me whole or just nibble off a few appendages, but I take a deep breath and say, "So...?"

She gives me that crocodile smile again. "My sources tell me you're quite the sleuth."

I kind of look down and shrug.

"So it should be no trouble at all for you, finding my dog."

I look up at her. "I wouldn't know where to start. I have no idea who took your dog!"

She buffs another claw and says, "Then you're just going to have to start *getting* some ideas, aren't you, Samantha?"

I took a deep breath and let it out as I said, "Mrs. Landvogt, look. I spent the whole night chasing around for Marique. Nobody saw her...there was no sign of her anywhere. Now we find out that someone's dognapped her. Don't you think you should call the police?"

The paper flew open in my face. "They'll kill her!"

"But—"

"And I'm not going to pay fifty thousand dollars for something that already belongs to me!"

"But—"

"You...!" She clenched her claws and vacuumed air through her nostrils. "You are going to find her and you are going to bring her home."

"I could try..."

She studied me a minute. "You shall do more than try,

you shall succeed!" That smile crept across her face again as she said, "And if you don't, I'll have no choice but to tell the authorities about your living situation."

All of a sudden it felt like I had a mouth full of Styrofoam. "My living situation?"

"Don't play dumb with me, Samantha. I know all about you, and if you don't want to find yourself on the street, you'll find my dog and you'll bring her home!"

I stood there for a minute with my heart whacking away and my hands going clammy. Finally I tried, "There's no law against me living with my best friend!"

She threw her little turban-head back and laughed. "Don't think for an instant I'm going to fall for that! I know you're living at the Senior Highrise, so let's stop playing games, shall we?"

All of a sudden I was on fire—pure, angry fire. It started in my cheeks and then spread through my body, and as I'm standing there burning up, I look the Crocodile square in the eye and say, "Fine! Go ahead and call! There's no way that your dog running off was my fault, and if you think you can blackmail me into finding her, you're wrong!"

And I'm marching straight for the door when I hear, "Too bad about your grandmother."

I froze.

"I don't think she'd do well on the streets in the dead of winter."

I turned around. "You can't do anything to her and you know it."

The Crocodile studied one of her nails. "Oh? I believe

she's been violating her lease for over a year now…" She looked straight at me. "With a few phone calls, that little apartment of yours could be occupied by any number of people on a very lengthy waiting list."

My mouth opened and closed, but no sound came out.

She smiled and said, "Hadn't you better run along? You have work to do."

I turned and walked out. And I slammed the door, all right, but as I stood there in the hallway, shaking, I knew there was no way around it.

I had to find that dog.

FIVE

Marissa and I spent the next hour locked in her room, trying to decide how to get me out of the mess I was in. But since I didn't really want to skip town or murder anybody, I finally decided to start digging for answers at the Pup Parlor.

Vera was in the middle of hosing down a schnauzer when I came clanking through the Pup Parlor door. She took one look at me, turned off the spray, and said, "Did you find her?"

I shook my head and said, "No."

"I should never have asked you to show her, Sammy, I'm sorry."

"It's not your fault, Vera, I—"

"But I know what a pain in the neck that woman is! Every time she brings Marique here, she's got to boss me around. The water's too cold, I've got the blower on too fast, I'm brushing her precious baby too hard. She makes me a nervous wreck."

"Holly told me about the business license. Can she do that?"

Vera wagged the nozzle in my direction. "Lilia Landvogt seems to be able to do whatever she wants."

"But you didn't even touch her dog!"

The schnauzer shook out all over her, but she didn't seem to care. She turned the water back on and started spraying him down some more. "That's the whole point. She says if I had been in charge, Marique wouldn't have run away. She's gotta blame someone, so she's blaming me."

Very quietly, I said, "She's also blaming me."

Vera looked over her shoulder at me. "But there's not much she can do to you."

I looked down.

She turned off the water and watched me toe some dog hair around the floor. "No...!" Finally she shakes her head and blasts the schnauzer with water again, muttering, "How does that woman find these things out?"

"Hudson says that money can start a pretty good fire, for paper that's green."

Vera snaps the water off again. "She's not bribing people, I can tell you that. Lilia Landvogt is as tight as a tailor. She's come back after four days and said, 'You didn't get the smell out,' and made me wash that prissy dog all over again."

"Did she pay you for it?"

"Are you kidding? She's always to the penny. I think I'd have heart failure if she ever tipped me."

I thought about this a minute. "So you don't think she'd pay fifty thousand dollars to get her dog back?"

"Fifty thousand...what?" The schnauzer drenched her again. She grabbed a towel. "What are you saying?"

"Marique's been dognapped. They want fifty thousand dollars for her."

A canary could've flown in Vera's mouth. "Fifty thousand dollars!" She dried off an arm. "That's unbelievable!"

I laughed. "Yeah."

She got the schnauzer out of the tub and said, "So why doesn't she call the police instead of threatening you?"

I helped towel the dog down and put him in a drying cage while I told her about the ransom note and how I had to find Marique.

She got the blower going and said, "This is ridiculous. She's ridiculous. How can she expect you to find her stupid dog? I have a good mind to call the police myself."

"You can't, Vera!"

She looked at me and sighed. "No, of course I won't."

"I was hoping that maybe you had some ideas."

"About who stole the dog?"

I nodded.

She shook her head. "Anyone that knows Lilia knows how nuts she is about Marique. And that she's got money."

"So you do think she'd pay it?"

"She's not real stable when it comes to that dog." Vera swatted some fur off her pants with the dog towel and laughed. "Maybe she just needs some grandchildren."

I tried to picture the Crocodile as a grandmother, but I couldn't see her shaking any kind of rattle that wasn't on the end of a snake. I sighed. "Vera, I have to find that dog. Do you have any idea who might have done it?"

Vera scowled. "Half this town could've. Who *wasn't* at the parade?"

I shook my head. "How am I ever going to find her? I've got nothing to go on!"

Vera started sweeping up. "Maybe Lilia's bluffing. Or maybe she'll cool off."

I watched her flick hair across the floor. "What about people who hate her?"

Vera threw back her head and laughed. "Land sakes! That's got to be a long list. And you can add me to it. After that noise about revoking my license...!"

I could feel a little tingle dancing around my brain. "It must've been real important for her to have Marique in the parade....I mean, it doesn't sound to me like she lets that dog out of her sight much."

"True..."

"And having Marique jump off the float right in front of the judges would've been really embarrassing if the cats hadn't kind of covered that up for her."

She studied me and said, "What are you getting at, Sammy?"

"I'm not sure...." I looked up at her and asked, "Where's Mr. Petersen's print shop?"

"Mr. Petersen! Why do you want to talk to that pill?"

I shrugged. "Maybe he has some ideas. About the other dog owners. They didn't seem too crazy about Marique being the star. Maybe one of them's behind this."

She picked up the dustpan and said, "His shop's out on West Main—six or seven blocks down. I don't think he works Sundays, although we are gettin' close to Christmas so he might be there. Why don't you call first?"

I grabbed the broom and helped her pick up the dog hair. "No, I think I'll just walk over there and check."

She gave me a worried look. "Why don't you take Holly

with you? She went out to get some Jell-O and soup for Meg, but she should be back fairly soon."

"Meg's still sick?"

"She's on the mend now, but that was one nasty bug." Vera scooped up the dustpan of hair and said, "Why don't you have a seat? Holly'll be back in a bit."

Now, I'm not very good at sitting and waiting, so I said, "I think I'll just head over there."

"I'd feel better if you waited."

"You're not afraid of him, are you?" I laughed and said, "I mean, how seriously can you take a guy who looks like a stinkbug?"

She practically spilled the dustpan. "A what?"

"A stinkbug. Didn't you think he looked like a stinkbug last night with those tails and that hair slicked back?"

All of a sudden she just busted up. And she laughed so hard that she wound up sitting on the floor with tears running down her cheeks. "A stink...a stinkbug!" She pushed the tears away and said, "I'm never ever going to be intimidated by Royce Petersen again. The next time he starts bossing me around I'll just tell myself...he's a big stinkbug!" That started her laughing all over again, so I said 'bye and clanked out the door.

The whole way up Main Street I tried to put a finger on that tingle in my brain, but it was like chasing an itch in the middle of your back—you scratch all around it and it kind of fades away, but you never really get it.

Now, the seven-hundred block was farther than I'd ever walked. Down West Main, anyway. And it's not that seven blocks is a long way to go, it's just that after about

Melvin's Jewelers in the one-hundred block, West Main starts going downhill in a hurry.

All along Main there are dingy little one-room shops. Carpet stores and bridal shops and travel agencies—and you wonder, who goes there? I mean, there are big carpet stores and bridal shops and travel agencies right up the street in the mall—who's going to get their wedding dress at a place where the mannequins are missing fingers and noses?

Petersen's Printing wasn't hard to find. It was the first shop past a service alley in an old two-story brick building. The windows were kind of milky with dirt and covered with burglar bars, and there were bamboo window shades resting cockeyed on stacks of books and papers.

The sign propped up in the window was dusty and torn, and said Closed. But there were some fluorescent lights on, so I tried the door anyway. It was locked. I whacked at the window with my knuckles and waited. I did it again, and waited some more. Then I peeked past the shades, but all I could see was a desk buried in papers. I decided to see if there was a back door somewhere.

The service alley didn't look too inviting. I mean, even though it was the middle of the day, no sunlight was getting in, and garbage seemed to ooze up through the gravel. And I had almost convinced myself to just try back later when I noticed a car parked in front of a roll-up door. I took a few steps down the alley, and when I got a good look at the car, I knew right off—it belonged to Mr. Petersen. It was shiny black with edges that were kind of rounded and side panels that half covered the wheels. It looked like a giant stinkbug.

I circled the car, wondering what a guy who worked in such a messy place was doing with such an immaculate vehicle. The bumpers were like mirrors, and the body didn't have a fingerprint on it.

I didn't mean to touch it. And I swear I only brushed against the bumper, but all of a sudden that car starts wailing and beeping like an ambulance. I jumped a mile in the air, and before I'd even had a chance to come down, the roll-up door whips open and there's Mr. Petersen, leveling a giant handgun right at my heart.

I threw my hands up in the air and said, "I'm sorry! I swear! I didn't mean to touch it!"

His eyes pinched closed a bit and he lowered the gun. "Well, well, well. If it's not the brain surgeon that lost the dog." He unlocked the car and turned off the alarm.

I guess my adrenaline was pumping pretty good, because my mouth popped off with, "Me? Who's the guy who kept right on driving?"

"Hey! Watch your mouth!" He tucked the gun inside the belt of his pants and muttered, "Like I don't get enough of this from the Wicked Witch."

"Uh...that would be Mrs. Landvogt?"

"You didn't hear that from me."

"What's she doing? Threatening to put you out of business, too?"

He eyed me like I was a guppy swimming around his toilet. "She's already pulled that one on me. What are you doing here, anyway?"

I ignored the question. "But you're still in business."

43

He kept eyeing me. "If you call slaving here twenty-four seven being in business, then yeah, I guess I am." He shook his head. "Look, kid, I don't know what you're nosing around here for, but if you got any brains at all you'll leave and not come back."

My brain was racing, trying like crazy to put some pieces together. "I'm...I'm not really nosing, it's—" All of a sudden something clicked. "It's just that anyone could figure out she's got something on you."

"And why do you say that?"

I scratched the back of my neck. "How else does a pedigree wind up on the cover of the Santa Martina calendar?"

I could tell by the look on his face that I had hit the bull's-eye. And it about made him short-circuit, because he says, "That witch sent you here to harass me! That's what you're doing here! Well, you can tell her it's a sad day when you have to send a kid to do your dirty work. You can also tell her it's not going to work. I'm not caving in to her anymore!" He went back inside, and I could see the grip of his gun sticking out of his waistband as he reached for a large chain dangling from the door. He yanked on it, and as the door rumbled down he yelled, "Get away from my shop, you hear me? And don't ever come back!"

As I watched the door clang closed, I realized that any chance I'd had of getting information out of him was gone.

Royce Petersen had just flushed me down the drain.

SIX

I thought about going back to the Pup Parlor to tell Vera what had happened, but there was so much stuff jumbling around in my brain that I needed a minute to think. So instead, when I got to Broadway, I looked both ways for Officer Borsch, then jaywalked across the street.

I cut across the grass to the Senior Highrise and started up the fire escape, and for the first two flights I thought about Mr. Petersen and his temper and how scary he looked with that gun in his hand. But the farther away from him I got, the safer I felt, and by the time I was on the fifth floor, my stomach wasn't flipping with fear anymore, it was hungry.

So my brain was busy putting together a gigantic ham and cheese sandwich when I got to our hallway and remembered—no Mrs. Graybill to worry about. For once I got to go trucking down the hall and open the apartment door like I lived there.

Grams was still dressed in her church clothes. She whispered, "Hello, Samantha," over the receiver of the phone, then said, "That's why the gal in Outpatients switched me over to you." She listened for a minute. "Well, when is *he* supposed to be in?...When do you *think* he'll return?"

She closed her eyes and shook her head. "Fine. I'll try around two o'clock."

She got off the phone and said, "They've lost her. Nobody seems to have any idea where she is."

"Who?"

"Daisy!"

That sounded like good news to me.

Grams looped an apron over her head. "I've been on the phone for forty-five minutes and all they can tell me is that she's been released. They won't give me any details because I'm not family, and they don't seem to care that a friend might want to see how she's doing."

"A *friend*?"

"Oh, Samantha, come now. The woman was hurt—the least I can do is check in on her." She tied the apron behind her and said, "Maybe she's on her way home now."

I didn't want to tell her that the last thing we needed was for Mrs. Graybill to come home. I mean, Mrs. Graybill would probably sign over her Social Security check to Mrs. Landvogt if it meant getting rid of me. And the more I thought about it, the more I knew that I really couldn't tell Grams about *any*thing. If I let on about us being the entrée on La Croc's supper menu, she'd go into hyperworry and self-destruct before the day was out.

And thinking about the mess Grams was in because I had to live with her, well, I kind of lost my appetite for that gigantic ham and cheese. So when she dug a can of chicken gumbo out of the cupboard and said, "Sound good?" I just nodded and got busy making toast.

And I was hanging over the toaster, watching the wires

glow, thinking about what Grams and I would do if Mrs. Landvogt *did* turn us in, when the phone rang.

Grams picked it up, and for the longest time she just stood there with her eyes expanding to fill up her owl glasses. Finally she said, "Lana, Lana, slow down! NBC? Okay! That's wonderful. We'll tune right in." She got off the phone and cried, "She did it!"

Grams rushed into the living room to turn on the TV, but I froze. I mean, Lady Lana had dumped me at Grams' because she didn't feel like being a mom anymore. She felt like being a movie star. And in the beginning when she'd call and say she'd come back soon, I couldn't wait. I missed her. But it didn't take long to figure out that soon meant later and that she didn't really care about being with me. She cared about being a movie star.

And I'd gotten used to living with Grams—used to the couch and hiding my clothes. Used to sneaking in and out. Even used to Mrs. Graybill. And all of a sudden it hit me that I'd rather have to sneak past ten Mrs. Graybills every night than leave Grams to go live with my mom. And watching Grams flip the channels on the TV, I realized that this was it. It didn't matter what Mrs. Landvogt did to me. My mother had made it, and my time with Grams was up.

I stumbled into the living room, feeling like the air was too heavy to breathe. "Is she in a movie?"

"No, a commercial! She says there's great money in commercials and seems to think it's a real foot in the door." She beamed at me. "Isn't this exciting? Your mother's going to be on TV!"

I sat down on the couch, trying to remember the last time I'd seen Grams so excited. "What's it a commercial for?"

"She wouldn't say. But she says it's okay to laugh—that it's supposed to be funny."

I didn't feel like laughing. I felt like crying. Grams sat next to me and patted my knee. "Are you all right?"

I forced up the corners of my mouth and nodded, and we sat there together, staring at the TV.

And then all of a sudden there she was, for the first time in over a year, my mother. She walked toward me on TV and smiled like only Lady Lana can smile. Then she stopped, and what came out of her mouth was, "Everybody gets gas."

I held my breath and covered my face with my hands. And as I'm peeking through my fingers, she says, "But sometimes when gas pressure gets too much, I can feel like this..." and there goes her body, blowing up like a hot air balloon. "When that happens, I take GasAway, and feel better." She holds up a box of GasAway, shrinks back to normal, then smiles at the camera and says, "Try it, when you feel like this..." and her body blows up like a zeppelin again, "...and you'll feel better!" She shrinks back, and then all of a sudden she's gone.

Grams and I just sat there, blinking at the television. Finally Grams says, "Well, I suppose it's a start."

I got up and turned off the TV. "My mother, the Gas-Away Lady."

"Samantha, come on, now. She's been working hard to get a part."

"In a movie! In a sitcom! Even in a soap. But in a commercial for *GasAway*?"

The phone rang. Grams took a deep breath and said, "That's probably her now. Let's be positive, all right? She's very excited about it and I don't think we should discourage her. She understands the business better than we do, and who knows? Maybe she really can parlay this into a part in a movie or a TV show."

Grams went into the kitchen to answer the phone, and I snuck out the door. There was no way I could congratulate the GasAway Lady—not with the upset stomach she'd just given me.

* * *

I wound up at Hudson's. Not to talk, just to sit on his porch and try to forget. Trouble is, you can't really space out when you're with Hudson. To him, spacing out is like using a Swiss army knife to dig holes.

Hudson took one look at me and said, "Ooooo. You've had a rough one."

"I'm not talking about it."

He pulled on an eyebrow.

"I'm not."

"Well, have some tea, then, and tell me what you've decided to do about Heather."

"Heather! I haven't even had a chance to *think* about Heather. What I'm going to do about her is nothing."

"Nothing?"

I threw my head back and groaned. "What can I do? What's it matter, anyway? If she's got nothing better to do than throw cats at floats, that's her problem."

Hudson dusted off a boot. "Wow, you must be in a stew."

"You can say that again."

"I mean a *real* stew. For you not to care about Heather?"

The truth is, I did care. But I hadn't had time to think about her, and compared to the other monsters in my life, well, she seemed like the runt of the litter. I sighed and said, "What can I do about it, anyway?"

Hudson smiled into the distance. "Oh, I don't know..."

I studied him. "What are you thinking?"

"Oh, nothing. Nothing that you'd be interested in, anyway."

"Hudson!"

"So...?"

"So all right, I'm interested! I just don't have any time."

He laughed. "This wouldn't take any time."

I sat up. "So, let's hear it."

He smoothed down an eyebrow and eyed me. "Ever hear of 'The Tell-Tale Heart'?"

I groaned. "By Edgar Allan Poe?"

"That's the one."

"Heather hasn't got a conscience."

"Sure she does," he said with a chuckle. "You've just got to help dig it up."

"How am I supposed to do that?"

He smiled. "Be her conscience for her. Remind her with everything you do that you know what she's done. A guilty soul cannot keep its own secret."

"She hasn't got a soul, either. Besides, she probably doesn't even care if I know or not."

Hudson chuckled. "She would if she thought you were plotting revenge."

"Revenge? Hudson, you don't understand...I don't have *time* to plot revenge."

He gave me that smile again. "The revenge will take care of itself. All you have to do is set the stage."

"Hudson!"

"Okay. Tell me this—what's your demeanor when you're around Heather? Are you friendly? Are you hostile?"

"I usually just avoid her."

"You're not confrontational?"

"No."

"Sociable?"

"No. I just try to steer clear of her."

He smiled. "What if your behavior toward Heather changed radically? What if you were, for example, really nice to her?"

I thought about this a minute. "She'd probably wonder what I was up to."

"Now let's play with the opposite scenario. What if you acted like you were plotting to get her? Really get her."

I laughed and said, "That would definitely make her nervous, but c'mon, Hudson—she's not going to admit she catapulted cats just because I make her a little nervous."

"Remember 'The Tell-Tale Heart.'"

"That's only a story."

He went back to tugging on an eyebrow. "It's your job to make it reality."

I took a deep breath and looked out at the sky. "I'll think about it."

"Thatta girl!" He filled up my tea and said, "So how'd it go with Elyssa today?"

I sat up. "Oh! I forgot!"

He *tsk*ed at me and said, "Some best friend."

"Hudson, give me a break. I've had a horrible day."

He grinned into the distance. "Still don't want to talk about it?"

"No."

"Then why don't you go over to Elyssa's?"

"Are you trying to get rid of me?"

"Never, Sammy! But I think she might be waiting for you."

I studied him. "Why do you think that?"

He shrugged. "I saw her on my way to church. She was kind of perched on a windowsill, looking outside."

"So?"

"So she was still there when I came home."

I got up. "You're kidding."

"Nooo."

"I'd better go."

I ran down the steps and he called, "Think about 'The Tell-Tale Heart'!"

* * *

Elyssa wasn't sitting on the windowsill. She was leaning on it with her elbows, holding her face in her hands. She jumped up as I came up their walkway, and even though I couldn't hear her, I could tell she was calling, "Mom, she's here, she's here!"

The door flew open before I had a chance to knock.

Mrs. Keltner stood behind Elyssa, drying her hands on a towel. "You have just made a little girl's day."

Elyssa grabbed my hand. "You'll never guess what!"

I laughed. "What?"

"You get to take me to the park!"

"I do?"

Elyssa's mom laughed and said, "Only if you have time, and only if you want to."

I looked at Elyssa, beaming like the sun, and all of a sudden I forgot about my mother and Mrs. Landvogt and her stupid dog. I grinned at her and said, "Sure."

Elyssa jumped up and down, squealing, "Let's go!"

The Elf Mom said, "Wait a minute, sweetheart, we had a deal. You go in there and finish your lunch, and then you can go." She looked at me. "Can I offer you some macaroni and cheese?"

God could have asked to have a word with me right then and I would've said, Excuse me, I gotta go have some macaroni and cheese first. I nodded, and the next thing you know I was shoveling away.

Elyssa finished before I did. She said through a mouthful, "I'm ready!"

Her mom laughed. "Go wash up." The minute Elyssa was out of the room, she pulled up a chair and said, "Sammy, I can't tell you how grateful I am that you came over. I haven't seen her this happy since, well...in ages." She leaned forward and whispered, "Now I've been thinking—and I don't want Elyssa to know the details, all right?—but I'm willing to give you baby-sitting money for spending time with her."

I shook my head and gulped down some milk. "I don't mind taking her to the park."

"Hear me out, Samantha. I'm at my wits' end. I've tried and tried to find out what's going on with her, but she won't talk about it, she won't cry about it—even when I know she's upset, she never cries." She let out a heavy sigh. "I've made arrangements for Elyssa to have a psychological evaluation, but the woman who's been recommended to me isn't available until after Christmas. I don't worry about Elyssa when she's at school, and I don't worry about her once we're home, but there's an hour between the time her school lets out and the time I get off at the home. She's supposed to walk straight over to the nursing home to meet me after school, but sometimes she gets...distracted." She looked down the hall to make sure Elyssa wasn't coming back. "What school do you attend?"

"William Rose."

She looked relieved. "You're right around the corner from her. She goes to Landview. Would you pick her up and walk her over to the nursing home after school? It's right there on Sycamore, a block off Main."

"Behind the supermarket?"

She nodded. "It would just be until Christmas break."

My stomach was feeling pretty happy, and it must have affected the rest of me, because out of my mouth pops, "Sure."

She lets out a huge sigh. "Thank heavens."

Elyssa comes charging up the hallway, calling, "I'm ready!" so I thanked Mrs. Keltner for lunch, and before you know it I'm on my way to the park with the Elf.

And the funny thing is, I had fun. A lot of fun. I chased her down the tube slide and trapped her in the jungle gym. We twirled on the bars until we were both so dizzy we didn't know which way was up, and I even rode a swing on my stomach. I didn't think about the GasAway Lady or "The Tell-Tale Heart," or even the Crocodile— I just had fun.

But somewhere on the walk home it all came flooding back. And by the time I had dropped the Elf off, I knew that I had to pay the Crocodile another visit.

And this time, *I* would be the one asking the questions.

SEVEN

There was a bright red Jeep parked in the circular drive. And I would've thought it was Tina's, only the license plate said SKI BOY. There were sunglasses on the dash, some flags and a fancy-looking megaphone on the backseat, and on the floor were a sack of oranges and a couple of blankets.

I was still kind of studying the Jeep, trying to figure out who Ski Boy might be, when Tina answered the door. "Well, if it isn't Little Miss Gumshoe. Didja find her?"

I stepped inside, and the door closed with a *bo-beep* behind me. I asked, "What *is* that sound?"

She looked puzzled. "What sound?"

"You know...that *bo-beep* sound."

She laughed and said, "Oh, that. That's our rip-roaring security system. Anytime you open a window or door, *be-boop,* there goes the alarm. And when you shut it, *bo-beep!* There it goes again."

"That's all it does?"

"When it's in the Home mode, yeah." She rolled her eyes. "Mother calls it the annunciator, but to me it's the Tattler." She whispered, "Can't get away with anything around here!"

Now, I knew there was something different about her,

but it didn't hit me until I'd followed Tina through the house that she was drunk. She stopped in the doorway of the sitting room and rolled her eyes again. "Good luck breakin' the two of them up. They're talking *money*."

The Croc was sitting in a wheelchair with her leg propped up, swirling ice cubes in a glass, and she was laughing. Really laughing. And with all those teeth showing, let me tell you—it was a scary sight. Like someone sharpening knives at a playground.

The guy she was talking to was blond and really tan, and he was swirling ice and laughing, too. He says, "Lilia, you're too much!"

The Croc laughs some more, then, without taking her eyes off him, she reaches her glass out and says, "We need refills, Tina."

Tina waves and says, "Over here, Mother…hel-lo. Hate to break up the party, but you've got company, and if you'll recall, Buddy and I have plans."

The Croc looks over and practically drops her glass. "What the devil are you doing here?"

I try to stare her down. "I've got some questions."

Everyone's quiet for a minute, then Buddy raises an eyebrow in Tina's direction. She says, "Oh. This is Mother's private eye."

His other eyebrow goes up, and you can tell he's dying to bust up. But instead, he stands, gives the Croc a little bow, and says, "It was so nice meeting you, Lilia. I've learned more today than I have in the last three and a half years at the university. Maybe we can continue our conversation sometime."

"I'd be delighted," she says, and as they're leaving, calls, "Don't forget your jacket."

Buddy looks back, and sure enough, there's his turquoise ski jacket, sitting on the chair. The Croc jokes, "Couldn't lose you in a snowstorm in that thing...!"

Buddy laughs and says, "You're right about that," then thanks her again and disappears.

The alarm *be-boop*s as Buddy and Tina open the door, and the Croc waits for it to *bo-beep* closed. Then she turns on me and says, "I don't see my dog."

"I'm here to look at that video again."

She flicks her fingernails, one at a time. "And why do you need to do that?"

I look straight at her. "Do you want me to try to find your dog or not?"

"Don't be insolent! Of course I want you to find my dog! What kind of an idiotic question—"

"Then I need to see the video, and I need to see the calendar."

She studies me a minute. "I presume you mean the Canine Calendar?"

"That's right."

She points through a doorway. "Down the hall and to the right. It's hanging in the kitchen. I'll cue up the video."

The kitchen looked like the Fort Knox penny room. Copper pots and pans were hanging from the ceiling, from the walls—from everywhere. Even the three ovens were copper.

I saw the calendar right away, but I had to circle around

a large marble island to get to it. And I was so busy gawking at everything that before you know it I'd gawked my way clear past the island to the far side of the kitchen.

I peeked over some Dutch doors into another room, and right away I knew it wasn't someplace Mrs. Landvogt spent much time. There was no marble, no copper, no glass, and no chandeliers. Just a simple table with some folding chairs and a small TV. On the floor were two white ceramic bowls—one with water, one empty—and at the far end of the room was the back door to the house with a small doggy door in it.

I looked out a kitchen window at Marique's stomping grounds and was busy picturing Pomeranians playing golf when I heard, "Finding any clues, Samantha?"

I about shot through copper.

She laughed, then pushed a lever on the handle of her wheelchair and turned around. "You've got to work on those nerves if you're going to be a private eye."

I stuffed my heart back in my chest. "I don't want to be a private eye."

She zoomed off. "Sure you do."

I pulled the calendar from the wall and followed her to a room with a white marble fireplace and a TV the size of a movie screen. She got the video going and handed me the remote. "So what are you looking for?"

I fast-forwarded to the part where the cats went flying, then watched the dogs jump off the float in slow motion. Only three of the dogs went in the direction that Marique had jumped. One was a gray, kind of hairless dog with a tail like a whip, one had long legs and long hair and looked like a cross between an Afghan and a collie, and the third one was Hero. I flipped through the calendar until I found the hairless dog. It was on the July page, dressed in cowboy boots and a cowboy hat, sitting by a No Parking sign in front of the bus station. I checked the credits by the picture. *Dog: Ribs. Owner: Paula Nook. Photo: Paula Nook.*

I looked straight at the Crocodile. "What do you know about Paula Nook?"

She snickered and said, "She likes a good barbecue, and it shows."

"That's it?"

She eyed me like she wasn't sure if she wanted to show off her muscles. Finally she pulled a large black leather notebook from beside her in the wheelchair. She kept one eye on me as she thumbed through it, and when she'd found the right page she cleared her throat and flexed. "Paula Nook. 801 Braxton Way. Married twice, divorced twice. Has a daughter in Santa Luisa who's living with a rodeo washout. Owns a share of Palmer's Bar and Grill and waitresses there six nights a week. Declared income last year, fourteen thousand, two hundred dollars." She practically buffed her claws against her robe. "Next?"

I found the Afghan-collie on the August page. It was dressed like a clown, pawing at the fairground's gate. I held it up for the Croc and waited.

"That's Fiji. Nora Hallenback's dog." She flipped through her black book, saying, "She's married to Dr. Franklin Hallenback, has had three miscarriages, no children." She smoothed open the book. "Resides at 11018

Carriage Court. Can't balance a checkbook, allergic to nuts, smokes on the sly to keep her weight down. Does the usual doctor's-wife charity circuit." She looked up and chuckled. "If you ask me, Nora should've married an obstetrician instead of a psychiatrist—would've done her a lot more good."

The last one was Hero. I held the calendar open to October and she laughed. "Lance Gigoni wasted a lot of time getting him in that Halloween costume. That dog's a freak! They had a ceremony at the park to announce the winners for the calendar, and that dog tried to pee on his own tail! I think he thought it was a rat chasing him around."

"What about Mr. Gigoni?"

"Lance is your typical laborer. Got a bad back, always needs a bath." She found his page. "Out of work a lot. Sometime resident of a tenement building on South Elizabeth, but right now he's living in his truck because his wife threw him out of the apartment again. He hovers around a hundred. Maybe ninety-five."

"Ninety-five?"

"IQ points. As a matter of fact, none of those people have made it very high up the evolutionary ladder. Not even Nora."

I blinked at her a minute, wondering what rung crocodiles were on.

She smiled. "Well? Who else?"

I closed the calendar. "That's it."

"That's it? I was just starting to have fun."

Now it seemed to me that Mrs. Landvogt was acting

kind of strange. For a lady whose baby had been 'napped, anyway. "Fun?"

She jiggled what was left of her ice. "You're wasting time, you know."

"I'm just trying to find a place to start."

She eyed me like I was hovering around seventy, then snapped, "How could any of them have my dog? They were all on the float!"

I handed her the calendar. "Maybe they found Marique when they were chasing after their own dogs. Maybe they grabbed her for you, then realized what a pain in the neck you are and decided to make a quick fifty thousand instead."

"What?!"

My heart was racing so fast it was lapping itself. "Do you really expect people to do you favors? You go around threatening them and blackmailing them...and on top of that, you're cheap!"

"How *dare* you..."

"If Marique ever does come back, you'd better figure out how to wash her yourself, 'cause Vera's sure not going to touch her after the way you've been treating her..."

"That woman has no business telling you—"

"And Mr. Petersen! You blackmail him into putting Marique not only in the calendar but on the *cover*. And now the poor guy's down there sweating away on Sunday trying to keep his business from going under."

She sat there for a minute with her eyes bugging out, then took a deep breath and said, "If the man can't run his business without paying illegals under the table, he shouldn't be running a business." She straightened her robe. "He was a moron to tell you."

I tried not to let her see I was shaking. Very quietly I said, "He didn't."

She hesitated, then just about dislocated her jaw. "Why, you little..."

I handed back the remote. "If you'll excuse me, I've got work to do."

I let myself out, and as the alarm *bo-beep*ed behind me I felt like I was stuck in quicksand. The more I moved the deeper I sank, and at the rate I was going it wouldn't be long before I was completely swallowed up.

EIGHT

I hadn't given "The Tell-Tale Heart" much thought. I'd been too busy thinking about Mrs. Landvogt and Mr. Petersen, and mapping out how I was going to visit the three dog owners after school. There was no place in my brain for Heather Acosta.

Then I walked into homeroom. And I don't know why, but when I saw Heather nudge her friend Monet and giggle in my direction, I sat down in my seat and gave her an evil little smile—like I had something up my sleeve. Something big.

Her face pinched up and she said, "What?"

I didn't even blink.

"Hey, what's your problem?"

I just kept smiling.

When Mrs. Ambler was done with the Pledge and the announcements, she held up a small cardboard box and shook it. "Okay, class, it's time to pick Kris Kringles. Remember, you don't have to do much to be appreciated. A little note in the desk, a goody delivered through a friend—nothing expensive. It's the thought that counts. Friday we'll exchange gifts at the cafeteria party. No gift is to exceed five dollars." She shook the box and started at Marissa's end of the classroom. "Keep them to yourselves and remember, no swapping! If you get someone you don't know very well, this is a great way to make a new friend."

By the time she came up my row, there wasn't much left shaking around in that box of hers. I reached in and pulled out Rudy Folksmeir's name, and at first I thought, Oh, no! I mean, Rudy likes dirt. At least, that's all I ever hear him talk about. He and his friends go out dirt bike riding a lot, and he's always talking about how hard the dirt was or how soft it was, or about how awesome it is, blowing through clouds of dirt. Not only is dirt the main word in Rudy Folksmeir's vocabulary, it's also a big part of his wardrobe. It usually says DIRT somewhere on his T-shirt, he wears it on his shoes and his jeans, and if there aren't clumps of it hanging off of him somewhere, he just looks dirty. Like he ripped up a vacant lot on his way to school.

So while part of me is trying to figure out whether or not I should leave little Baggies of dirt in Rudy's desk, a tickle in my brain makes me look straight up at Heather Acosta and give her that evil little smile again.

Well, she does a double take. So I look back down at Rudy's name and then at her again.

She sits there blinking for a minute, then shoots out of her seat and says, "Mrs. Ambler! Mrs. Ambler, you have to do this again....I...I..."

Mrs. Ambler stops and says, "For heaven's sake, why?"

She stands there, trying to come up with a reason. Finally she says, "I...I got myself. And I think a couple other people did, too."

Mrs. Ambler hesitates, then says to the class, "Did anybody else get themselves?"

Nobody says a word.

"Hmm." Mrs. Ambler shrugs. "Well, I have one left over, because Renée's absent. Let's just switch yours with hers."

Heather says, "But..."

Mrs. Ambler looks her straight in the eye. "But what, Heather?"

Heather blinks at her a minute, but what can she do? Finally she says, "Nothing, Mrs. Ambler," and switches slips. And when she looks over her shoulder at me, I give her that little smile again and tuck Rudy's name in my folder.

Now, to tell you the truth, I had no idea what I was doing. But all day long I found myself going out of my way to follow Heather. Instead of avoiding her like I usually do, I'd run clear around buildings so I could walk behind her. And when she'd notice me, I'd just stare at her like I was going to get her.

By the end of the day, she was checking over her shoulder for me, walking faster and faster between classes, looking really unhappy.

Me, I was feeling like a bumblebee at a barbecue.

On my way home, I was so busy thinking about how amazing it was that what I'd done had freaked Heather out so much that I was a block past Landview Elementary before I remembered I was supposed to pick up Elyssa.

I ran back and found her sitting on the top step, waiting. And when she saw me coming, she grabbed her papers and lunchbox and came charging toward me, calling, "Sammy!"

I laughed and put out my hand, and the whole way to the nursing home she talked about the class hamster,

Snowball, and how this kid Shane had emptied the pencil sharpener into his cage and turned him all black. It seemed like in no time we were there, looking for Mrs. Keltner.

Elyssa tugged me past the reception desk and down the hall, saying, "C'mon! She's probably down here."

Now, I'd never been in a nursing home before, and really, I'd never given much thought to what they were like. But the minute we turned down the hall, it hit me that I didn't like the place. Not at all. And it wasn't because the walls were green or the plastic flowers were faded. It wasn't even the woman in the hallway with tubes in her arms yelling" at a cart of bedpans. It was the smell. Like antiseptic and chlorine sprayed over with lilacs.

I followed Elyssa down the hall, but I wasn't keeping up. Every time we passed an open room I had to stop and stare. I tried not to, but I couldn't seem to help it. Some of the patients were napping; some were staring out a window. Some of them were fat; some of them were skin over bones. But all of them looked kind of gray—like they hadn't actually felt the sun in years.

All of a sudden I wanted out of there. Fast. But Elyssa called, "C'mon, Sammy, she's right down here!" so I kept following her. And my brain was telling me, Hurry up so you can say good-bye and get out of here! but my eyes kept slowing me down, looking in the rooms.

And that's when I saw her.

At first I didn't believe it. I just stopped and stood in the hallway for a minute telling myself, Nah...it can't be! but then I took two steps back and looked in the room again.

Sure enough, there she was, half asleep, with a little stream of drool running down her cheek—Mrs. Graybill.

Her hair was matted, as usual, but her mouth wasn't smeared with lipstick and her eyes weren't on fire like they usually are when she sees me. They were just dull. I whispered, "Mrs. Graybill?" because I still wasn't really sure.

She licked her lips and blinked at me once, and then she closed her eyes. "Sammy."

I just stood there, staring.

Finally her eyes opened again, and for the first time since I met her she smiled at me. "It's nice of you to visit."

I felt like I was having a very strange dream. I took a step inside and whispered, "What are you doing here? I thought you broke your arm."

She pulled her cast from beneath the sheets and grumbled, "Doctors."

I took another step and said, "But I don't understand. Why are you here?"

Just then Mrs. Keltner walked in. She straightened Mrs. Graybill's covers and poured her some water. "Well, Daisy, look at this. It seems you *do* know somebody in town."

Mrs. Graybill sighed and said, "Just leave me be, would you?"

Mrs. Keltner patted her hand, then whispered to me, "It worked out well with Elyssa?"

I nodded.

"See me before you go, okay?"

She left, and I looked back at Mrs. Graybill. "Grams called over at the hospital trying to find out how you were doing. They wouldn't tell her anything because she's not family."

Mrs. Graybill nodded. "Well, that was nice of her."

"She'll be glad to know you're all right. You *are* all right, aren't you?"

She shrugged and sort of nodded, and then just looked at me.

I looked back, not knowing what to say. And it's funny, for all the trouble Mrs. Graybill has caused me you'd think I'd be glad she was stuck in a nursing home breathing in sterile lilacs, but I wasn't. Finally I asked, "Do you want Grams to pick up your mail or water your plants or something?"

Mrs. Graybill closed her eyes and shook her head. And after a couple of minutes of watching her lie there, I whispered, "Well, I'd better be going...."

An eye opened and she gave me half a smile. "Don't want to worry that grandmother of yours?"

I just toed the linoleum with my high-top, and when I turned to leave she said, "Oh, Samantha? There is something. Would you mind bringing me my robe sometime? These gowns are so scratchy."

I nodded. "Sure."

She sat up and pulled her apartment key off a ring and handed it to me. "It's hanging in the bathroom."

I took the key and asked, "Do you want anything else? Your slippers? Your lipstick?"

She pulled the sheets up around her. "Doesn't matter," she said, and rolled over.

I tiptoed out and practically tripped on Elyssa sitting on the floor around the corner. She stood up and said, "How do you know her?"

"She's my grandmother's neighbor."

"Oh."

Just then Mrs. Keltner came up, so I asked, "Why is Mrs. Graybill here?"

She cleared her throat a bit and said, "She isn't well, dear."

"But what's *wrong* with her?"

Mrs. Keltner let out a little sigh. "Sometimes when people get older they need a little help caring for themselves. That's why she's here, and that's why we're here."

"But…"

She eyed Elyssa like maybe I shouldn't be talking about this anymore, and then said, "Thanks again for bringing Elyssa over." She stuffed some money in my pocket. "I'll see you tomorrow, all right?"

Now, it's not that I didn't need the money. I didn't *want* the money. I took it out of my pocket and stuffed it right back in her nurse shirt. "See you tomorrow," I said, then called to Elyssa, "Don't let Shane put any paint in Snowball's water dish!"

She giggled. "I won't!"

I was on my way outside when Mrs. Keltner called after me, "Sammy! I almost forgot to ask you…" She came hurrying toward me. "You were on the dog float—do you by chance have any idea who threw those cats into the parade?"

"Um…I don't know, maybe."

She looked over both shoulders like she was afraid someone would hear. "If you do, you need to tell Officer Borsch."

"Why?"

"Gil is a very proud man, and I'm afraid they've been roasting him down at the station. There's this one fellow down there that I know from the time my husband was on the force. Andy's a real instigator, and he takes things too far. Apparently he had a huge poster made of Gil falling off the horse and hung it up in the ready room, and he brought in a cake that said 'Giddy-up!'—childish stuff like that."

I had to look away to keep from busting up. I wanted to say, Giddy-up! and fall down laughing, but instead I bit the inside of my cheeks and got busy toeing at the ground.

"I think Gil would feel a lot better if he could produce the people who threw the cats. He's got a lead that they were a group of girls about your age—have you heard anything?"

I almost just said no. I mean, Officer Borsch is someone I wouldn't wish on my worst enemy. At least that's what I'd always thought. But here I was, able to do just that, and suddenly I *wasn't* so sure. Finally I looked up at her and said, "I'll see what I can find out."

She smiled and said, "Oh, that would be wonderful!"

I hurried outside and stood there for a minute taking in deep breaths, trying to flush the lilacs out of my nose. A picture of Heather sweating under Officer Borsch's light-bulb went dancing through my brain, and it left a strange taste in my mouth. Like eating lima beans and licorice.

I shook off the thought and told myself to get going. I had lots of work to do and not much time. I took out the notes I'd made at the Landvogt mansion, then ran across Main Street to a gas station. On the posted map I found Braxton Way—it was a cul-de-sac a few blocks east of College Street, about half a mile away.

So off I went to visit Paula Nook and her hairless mutt, Ribs. And I guess I was so busy thinking about what I was going to say if she answered the door that I wasn't really noticing the scenery—or the pickup truck parked in front of Paula's home. Not until the dog inside the cab about broke his nose trying to charge through the window to get me, that is.

I jumped and ran, and as I looked over my shoulder it hit me—there was only one dog in the whole world that looked like that. I went back to the cab, and sure enough, it was Hero. For a minute I thought I was at the wrong place—that maybe I'd mixed up addresses. I put some distance between me and the truck and checked my notes. Hero belonged to Lance Gigoni on Elizabeth Street, not on Braxton Way. So what, I wondered, were he and Lance doing at Paula's?

I put my notes away and went up the walk to her house, thinking that the best way to find out was to just dive in and see. I stood at the front door for a minute, wondering if I should risk electrocution by ringing or knock through the rip in the screen. I decided to knock.

I could hear country music playing inside, and I wasn't real sure if anyone had heard my knock, so I did it again, only this time I pounded.

All of a sudden the music stopped. For a little while I heard footsteps shuffling back and forth inside, then the peephole flipped open and a great big blue eye said, "Yeah?"

"Ms. Nook?"

The eye blinked. "What do you want?"

I felt like telling her she'd won tickets to the rodeo so she'd at least open the door. "I...um...I need to ask you some questions."

The eye just stared. "About?"

"About the Christmas parade." I felt like I was talking to a wooden Cyclops.

"I got nothin' to say," she said, and slammed the peep-hole closed.

I stood there for a minute staring at the rip in the screen, thinking. Finally I got off the porch and walked around to the garage. I put my ear up to the door and listened, but I didn't hear any tortured dogs whining inside. I whispered, "Marique! Here, girl!" and then peeked over the backyard fence and did the same thing.

Now, the backyard was like a little corner of the city dump, and I was so amazed by all the junk that was piled up that I must have stared at it longer than I thought, because all of a sudden I'm being attacked. By Hero.

I scramble up the fence the best I can, and for a minute he just stands there, barking at me. Then he tries to figure out some way to lift his leg on me. So there I am, hanging onto a fence post for dear life, while he's dancing around, squirting away, trying to nail me with pee, when his master comes up and says, "That ought to teach you to go snooping around where you're not wanted." He whistles and calls, "C'mon, boy!" and then shuffles off in his dirty cowboy boots and jeans. Hero chases after him, whipping his little red rat around behind him, but I didn't let myself off the fence until I heard them grinding gears down the street.

Now, there was no way I was going to go knocking on the door again. I mean, maybe she only showed her one eye, but Paula Nook's got a shotgun behind her door, you just know it. And the last thing I wanted was to see it aiming at me through that peephole—that blue eye of hers was bad enough.

I decided to give up on Paula and Ribs, and I obviously wasn't going to get far with Lance and Hero either, so I headed out to Carriage Court to see if maybe Nora Hallenback and Fiji knew anything. But the closer I got to the Hallenbacks', the more useless going there seemed. What could she possibly know about Marique? And why would she even care about helping me?

All of a sudden I felt really panicky—like I was running through a swamp with a mama crocodile at my heels, and everywhere I turned, another set of jaws opened up to bite me.

NINE

There were no pickup trucks parked on Carriage Court. No broken screen doors, either. And when I found Nora Hallenback's house, I didn't have to go sniffing around the garage door—it was wide open.

There was a white Mercedes-Benz parked inside, and a lady with puffy red hair was going back and forth between the house and the car, unloading flower arrangements.

I walked partway up the driveway and called, "Mrs. Hallenback?"

She turned and said, "Yes?"

I stepped into the garage. "My name's Samantha and I'm writing an essay for my English class about the dogs in this year's calendar..."

"Really?"

I crossed my fingers and nodded. "And I was hoping I could interview you about Fiji."

She handed me a flower arrangement, then dived behind the driver's seat for another. When she came up, she gave me a little squint and asked, "Aren't you the one that was on the float with Marique?"

I nodded.

"What a mess, huh?" She closed the car door, then

headed inside the house. "I entered Fiji on a lark. It was a first, and it will definitely be a last."

I followed her. "Why's that?"

"Those people are insane!" She looked at me. "Well, okay, not all of them. But a lot of them act like their child has been chosen as the next Gerber baby."

I put my arrangement on the counter next to the others. "Yeah. Mrs. Landvogt seems like that."

She laughed. "Lilia! What a perfect example. And she *has* a child. A beautiful young lady. You'd think she'd channel her energies into promoting Tina instead of that prissy little dog of hers." She took out a spray bottle and began squirting the arrangements. "I'm sorry. Franklin's right. I tend to run off at the mouth when I shouldn't." She looked at me and smiled. "After all, you're the one who showed Marique. I was just under the impression that you got shanghaied into that. Am I wrong?"

I laughed and said, "No, that's exactly what happened."

She seemed relieved. "Well, good. My intuition is usually right; it's my execution that's sometimes lacking."

"What do you mean?"

She got back to spraying tiger lilies. "Sometimes I really put my foot in my mouth."

I laughed and said, "Well, you don't have to worry about that with me! I do that all the time. Besides, Mrs. Landvogt isn't exactly easy to like."

She glanced at me. "You do know her, then?"

I nodded. "I've been to her house. She's kind of scary."

"That she is. Very intimidating." She laughed and said, "You're a brave young lady to have gone over there."

I shrugged. "She seems to know everything about everybody."

"Oh?" She stopped spraying. "Such as?"

"Not gossip," I said, looking up at her. "More like facts."

She walked an arrangement over to the dining room table and turned it a few times, finding the best angle. Her mouth twitched into a smile as she asked, "And what did Lilia have to say about me?"

My heart was busy doing a war dance, but I tried not to let it show. "Don't worry about it. It's not like I'm going to put it in my report or anything."

She came a few steps closer. "Put *what* in your report?"

I toed at the tile floor with my high-top. "Look, maybe I could just ask you some questions about Fiji? Where is she, anyway?"

"Outside." She put her hands on her hips and said, "First I'd like to know what Lilia said."

"Really, Mrs. Hallenback, it doesn't matter."

"Tell me!"

I toed the floor some more, then mumbled, "She says you can't balance a checkbook. That you're allergic to nuts and smoke on the sly to keep your weight down. That you do a lot of charity work"—I looked up at her—"and that you've had three miscarriages."

Nora's eyes popped open and she gasped, "She told you that?"

I scuffed at the floor and mumbled really fast, "She also said that you should've married an obstetrician instead of a psychiatrist—that it would've done you more good."

"What?" She stared at me a minute with her mouth hanging open, then slammed a flower arrangement onto the mantel over the fireplace. She took another and slammed it on an end table.

"I...I'm sorry, Mrs. Hallenback. Like I said, it's not like something I would put in my report."

She spun around. "The nerve of that woman! And after all I've done for her!"

"After what you've done for her?"

Her hands flew onto her hips. "Fifteen years ago when she came into town, Lilia Landvogt was a nobody with a five-year-old daughter and a pocket full of life insurance money. I hooked her up with a friend of Franklin's who helped her invest her money. She made an absolute killing on some stocks she bought, and now she's in that mansion on East Jasmine acting like the queen. Besides connecting her with Franklin's broker, I'm the one who assimilated her into society. Do you know how many times I've had that woman over for a dinner party? Do you know how many functions she's been invited to because I suggested we include her on the list? She would be nowhere in this town if it weren't for me!" She whipped a towel over the kitchen counter. "Well, that does it."

"Pardon me?"

Flames about shot from her eyes. "As far as I'm concerned, Lilia Landvogt can sit in that gaudy mansion and rot." She started flipping through an address book, saying, "I'm sorry. I'm sure this is not what you wanted for your report. Why don't you come back some other time. Right now I've got some phone calls to make." She turned her back on me and started punching in numbers, so I just let myself out the garage door.

On the way home I thought about Nora Hallenback burning up the phone lines, blacklisting the Crocodile, and it hit me that either Lilia Landvogt was going to be very sorry she'd ever tried to blackmail me…

Or I was going to be *dead* by the end of the week.

* * *

I hadn't even thought about Mrs. Graybill until I turned down our hallway. Then I remembered where she was and how I was supposed to deliver her robe. I stood at her door a minute with the key in my hand, but it felt weird. Like by having permission to be there I was breaking some ancient tradition. I decided to check in with Grams first.

The minute I walked through the door, Grams jumped out of her chair and said, "Samantha! I'm so glad you're home. I've got wonderful news!"

Somehow I knew this had to do with the GasAway Lady. "Uh-oh."

She slapped the couch and said, "Sit, sit!"

I sat.

She held my hand. "Your mother's coming home!"

I felt like my stomach was climbing up a roller-coaster track. "For good?"

"For Christmas."

There went my peanut butter and jelly, loop-de-loop. "Ho ho ho."

"Samantha…!"

"Well, what am I supposed to say to her? 'Hi, Mom. Long time no see. Gee, I'm glad you've got that gas problem under control'?"

"Sweetheart, she's your mother. When you see her, you two will work it out."

"And where's she going to stay? Here? I can't exactly see her sleeping on the floor."

Grams took off her glasses and started buffing them with the hem of her skirt. "We'll make room."

I studied her a minute. "Oh, I get it. She gets the couch and *I* get the floor."

Grams popped the glasses back on her nose. "Never mind about that now. The important thing is, she's coming home."

I rolled my eyes. "I can see the headlines now: GasAway Lady Returns to Santa Martina—Brings Lifetime Supply to Senior Highrise."

"Samantha, that's enough. Show some respect!"

I closed my eyes and whispered, "I don't want to talk about her, okay?" I took a deep breath and said, "I thought you might want to know—I found Mrs. Graybill today."

"You *found* her? Where?"

"In a nursing home."

"A nursing home! How on earth…? How did you find out?"

"Elyssa's mom works there."

"Elyssa? Oh, that's the girl you're walking home?"

"Right." So I told her all about the home and how I'd run into Daisy half-asleep in her bed. And when I started

talking about how awful the place smelled and how everyone in there looked so gray, she pinched her eyes closed
and shook her hands in the air to shut me up. Finally she
whispered, "What on earth is she doing in a nursing
home?"

"I don't really know. All Mrs. Keltner would say was
that she's not well. I don't think she wanted to talk about
it in front of her daughter." I held up Mrs. Graybill's key.
"She asked me to bring her her robe."

"*Daisy* did?"

So I told her all about what Mrs. Graybill had said and
how it felt really strange, her asking me to help her out. I
turned the key over in the palm of my hand. "Would you
come with me?"

She nodded. "Of course."

I don't know why, but we tiptoed down the hall. And
the minute we were inside her apartment we looked at
each other and kind of shivered. Grams whispered, "This
is so eerie," and it was. The apartment was laid out just
like Grams', but it didn't feel a thing like it. Everything
was faded. Old and faded. Like it had been left out in the
sun too long, only you could tell—it had been left in the
dark too long.

In the living room there was one chair, one couch, and
an old television. Next to the couch was a basket of wool
with crochet hooks, and across the back of the couch was
a five-inch stack of afghans. I pulled them back, one at a
time. There were dozens of them, all beautifully made.
All colorful. It felt like I'd uncovered a vein of gold in a
coal mine.

Grams whispered, "We shouldn't snoop."

I mumbled, "I'm not snooping, Grams."

She pulled on my arm and said, "We should get that robe and get out of here."

So I went into the bathroom and sure enough, there was her dirty pink robe, hanging on the door. I took it off the hook, and when I came back out I did a double take. There was my grandmother in Mrs. Graybill's bedroom, snooping.

"Grams!"

She jumped and then said, "Look at this."

It was a black-and-white photograph of two girls in floppy hats with their arms around each other, laughing. Grams pointed to the taller girl and whispered, "That's Daisy."

I held a corner of the frame and said, "No way!" I mean, the girl was about seventeen with long shiny hair and narrow ankles. Now, I've seen Mrs. Graybill's ankles. A million times. There's no way the ankles in that picture belonged to her.

Grams whispered, "She was beautiful, wasn't she."

I looked at the laughing eyes in the picture and said, "That can't be her!"

"Oh, it is. I'm sure of it. Look at the teeth. Look at the cheekbones. That's Daisy." She pointed to the other girl in the picture. "And I would bet this is her sister."

I stared at the photograph for a long time, and it struck me how the name Daisy fit the girl in the photograph. Like springtime. Like sunshine. It just fit her. And as I handed it back to Grams, I wondered how the Daisy in the picture had turned into the crabby old woman that I knew.

All of a sudden I wanted out of there. I whispered, "C'mon, Grams. Let's go."

It wasn't until I was locking up the apartment that I noticed Grams still had the photograph. She handed it to me and said, "I think maybe Daisy would like to have this, too."

I was still wrapped up in thinking about Mrs. Graybill when we got back to our apartment and heard the phone ringing. Grams hurried to answer it, then called, "Samantha? It's for you."

I put down Mrs. Graybill's stuff and headed into the kitchen. "Is it Marissa?"

Grams frowned and shook her head. "It's Mrs. Landvogt." She covered the receiver and whispered, "What ever happened about her dog?"

My knees were shaking before I even took the phone. "I'll tell you later," I said.

I put the phone up to my ear like it might hurt me. After all, I had whacked a stick at a hornet's nest when I'd been at Mrs. Hallenback's. There wasn't much chance I could avoid getting stung.

TEN

I didn't have to say hello. She knew I was there. "You've got until Friday," she snapped.

"Friday?" I whispered. "That's not enough time!"

"Friday's a luxury! Those goons called and demanded the money *tomorrow,* but I managed to put them off until Friday. I want to know everything—who you've talked to, what you've found out—everything."

I looked over my shoulder at Grams. "Uh…that's not possible right now."

She was quiet for a second and then said, "Ah…you haven't told your grandmother about our little arrangement."

"That's right."

"Then come over so we can talk."

"I could probably do that tomorrow after school."

"You'll do it now!"

I looked at Grams, watching me. I said, "I'll see you around four o'clock tomorrow," and hung up.

Before Grams could grill me, I crossed my fingers and said, "She wants me to help distribute flyers about her dog."

"It never came back?"

I shook my head.

Grams took some snapper out of the refrigerator and said, "That's a shame. I hope she gets it back."

I took down the rice and a measuring cup, thinking that that was the understatement of the century.

*　*　*

I didn't sleep very well that night. My brain was too busy trying to move through quicksand. I thought about Lance Gigoni and Paula Nook and stupid ol' Hero trying to pee on me. I thought about Mrs. Hallenback and her tiger lilies, and I wondered how many people she'd already called and told about the Crocodile. Then I thought about Mr. Petersen. How he'd yelled at everyone at the parade and how he'd probably yelled just the same at the illegals working in his print shop. And lying there in the dark, thinking about cranky ol' Mr. Petersen, I wondered if there was a picture on his dresser of him looking young and happy. And somewhere between thinking about Mr. Petersen and the Crocodile and Mrs. Graybill at seventeen, I realized that I had to figure out *why* they had turned out the way they had.

There was no way I ever wanted to look back at a picture of myself at seventeen and not recognize me.

*　*　*

I wasn't thinking about Rudy Folksmeir or dirt or even Heather Acosta when the alarm went off. I was thinking about sleep. I felt like I had spent the night trying to run, but in my dreams I couldn't even lift my legs. I dragged through breakfast and getting ready for school, and it

85

wasn't until Grams was shoving me out the door that I remembered Mrs. Graybill's robe.

I hurried back inside and stuffed it with the picture in a paper sack. Grams said, "Why don't you let me take it over?" which made sense, but something about it didn't feel right. So I said, "No, Grams. I told her I would." Then, as I'm charging down the hall again, I remember Rudy. "Oh no!"

"What is it?"

"Rudy Folksmeir! I'm his KK, and I'm supposed to bring him something. I completely forgot!"

"A present?"

I started digging through cupboards. "Just some kind of snack or something."

"How about a few shortbreads?"

I gave it a nanosecond. Pecan shortbreads are dry and crumbly—the closest thing to dirt we had in the house. I threw a few in a Baggie, kissed Grams good-bye, and flew out the door.

When I got to homeroom, I snuck them on Rudy's desk and then noticed that someone had put a beautiful Christmas tree cupcake on Heather's. Now, I don't know why, but my feet walked me right past my own desk, and before you know it, there I was, sitting at Heather's.

When Holly walked through the door, I motioned her over. She sat down in the desk next to me and whispered, "Why are you sitting in Heather's seat?"

I grinned. "I'm just warming it up for her."

Then Marissa walked in, so I waved her over, too. She said through her teeth, "What have you got—a death wish?"

Then Heather walked in. I stood up slowly and stared at her.

"Hey! What do you think you're doing?"

I just kept staring her down.

"Get away from my desk!" She looked at me, then at the cupcake, then threw the cupcake in the trash. Just like that. *Thunk.*

I glared at her some more, then opened my desk.

She pushed it back down. "You don't think I'm stupid enough to let you poison me, do you?"

I leaned forward and made a tick-tocking sound with my tongue, then I gave her that evil little smile and whispered, "It's almost time...!"

The tardy bell rang. And Heather must've thought it was a bomb going off, because she about spiked the ceiling, then threw her hand on her heart like she was trying to keep it from popping out of her chest. She gave me a really dirty look and turned her back on me, but all through homeroom her eyes kept darting in my direction.

I didn't notice until I was getting my books out of my desk that I got a present, too. An ornament. It was a white angel dangling from a red ribbon, and at first I didn't realize that it was made out of uncooked noodles. A piece of manicotti for the body, a piece of bow-tie pasta for the wings, and macaroni for the arms. The face was painted with a felt-tip marker and looked like it was caroling.

I peeked around the classroom to see if anyone was giving away that they were my KK. I figured I could eliminate boys right off. I mean, no boy would be caught dead leaving pretty painted pasta in someone's desk.

Brandy Cavaletto was looking in my direction, and she looked away, all right, but she might have been checking out Derrick Stern next to me. It was hard to say.

Tawnee Francisco smiled at me, but she didn't look *caught* or anything. And besides, Tawnee smiles at everyone. Cassie Kuo was looking at me through her bangs, but Cassie's kind of shy and always looks at people that way. Even when she answers questions, she does it right through her bangs.

Then there was Monique Halbig, staring straight at me. And the minute I caught her eye, she gave me a fluttery little smile and looked away. So I figured, okay. It was probably Monique. I took one last look at the pasta angel, put it in a safe corner of my desk, and closed the lid. Then I went back to staring at Heather.

After homeroom I followed her again. All day. And any chance they got, Marissa and Holly did it too, giving her steady, angry stares. And whenever she'd see me, I'd make that tick-tocking sound—like the crocodile in *Peter Pan* stalking Captain Hook. Then I started doing it *before* she spotted me, which worked even better. She'd hear me ticking, then grab on to Tenille or Monet like they were buoys in the ocean, and dive into a classroom.

At lunchtime we caught Dot up on what had happened that morning, and we all agreed that we should keep harassing Heather. So we went into the cafeteria to make her nervous from across the room, but she wasn't there. We checked the patio tables, but she wasn't there, either. Finally we split up. Holly and Dot went to look behind the bleachers, and Marissa and I went to check the locker room.

The side door to the locker room was wide open, so we tiptoed in, and right away I knew they were there. I could smell the cigarette smoke. We sneaked past two sections of showers, then ducked into an alcove of lockers. There was a full-length mirror across the corridor, and we could see the reflection of Heather huddled up in a corner with Tenille and Monet, passing a cigarette around. Heather was saying, "She knows. I tell you, she knows!"

"So what?" Monet squeaked back. "What can she do about it?"

Tenille laughed at Monet and said, "You don't know Sammy very well, do you?"

Heather dragged on the cigarette, then passed it to Monet. "She's working on something. Something big."

Monet took the cigarette. "Oh, what's she gonna do— put acid in your gel?"

I looked at Marissa like, Oooo, that's a good one! and she about busted up.

"I'm talking something big. Really big." Heather took the cigarette back from Tenille and whispered, "I think she's planning to kill me."

They both blinked at her. "*Kill* you?" Monet added, "Like with a knife or something?"

"I don't know! How am I supposed to know? She's act-ing so weird!" ·

Tenille snickered. "Yeah, even for Sammy."

Monet shook her head. "*Kill* you? Isn't that kinda like...drastic?"

"Well, *you* tell me what she's up to, then!" Heather snuffed out the butt. "She's way over the edge, and I'll tell you what—I'm staying away from her. Miles away from her. Don't wait for me between classes—don't even look for me at lunch. I'm going to eat in the library or in Mr. Caan's office…somewhere she'd never think to look for me. I'm not going to go anywhere I usually go—I'm going to do the opposite."

Tenille said, "She's still gonna find you."

I thought Heather was going to strangle her. "I just want to make it to Christmas, okay? After Friday I won't have to worry about her for three whole weeks. By then she should've forgotten about it."

They started moving in our direction, so we scrambled to the back of the alcove and held real still as they walked past us. When they'd ducked out the door, Marissa said, "She sure is feeling guilty about something."

I nodded. "And if it's not the cats, I don't know what it is."

Marissa said, "Okay, so how are we going to get her to crack?"

I could feel an idea start to tingle in the back of my brain. "Do you still have a Polaroid camera?"

Marissa rubbed her hands together. "Oooo! You've got a plan! Tell me!"

So I gave her a rough sketch of what I was thinking and then said, "Let's go find Holly and Dot. This is going to take all of us!"

We ducked out of the locker room, met up with Holly and Dot, and by the time the end-of-lunch bell was ringing, we had a plan that—with a little help from Officer Borsch—would make *anyone* rip up floorboards.

Even Heather.

* * *

After school I made myself forget about Heather and concentrate on what I was going to tell Mrs. Landvogt. I picked up Elyssa, and when I got to the home I was chickening out about seeing Mrs. Graybill again. It was too weird. But Mrs. Keltner wouldn't deliver the things for me. She said, "You've got to go in and see her. Just for a minute."

"But I—"

"Please, Sammy. She's been asking for you. She won't eat. She's pretty despondent. I think it'll help."

So I went in. And Mrs. Graybill took one look at me and let out a long sigh. "Samantha..." she said, like I was her long-lost friend.

I laid her robe across the foot of her bed and whispered, "Hi, Mrs. Graybill."

She wiped the drool from her cheek, then motioned to the chair next to her bed. "Sit, sit!"

I didn't want to sit. I wanted to give her her stuff and get away from there. Away from the lilacs and chlorine. Away from the gray.

She noticed there was still something else in the bag. "What have you got there?"

"Oh, I hope you don't mind....Grams thought you might like to have this."

She took the picture, and for a minute there I thought the Mrs. Graybill I knew was going to jump right out of bed and smash the thing over my head. Instead, she buried her face in her hands and started crying.

I whispered, "I'm sorry!"

She took another look at the picture, then hugged it to her chest, sobbing.

I didn't know what to do. I stood there like an idiot, watching her matted head bob up and down, wishing I'd never brought the picture. Finally I said, "I can put it back if you want."

She hugged it tighter and looked almost scared. "No!"

"But..."

She looked at the photograph again, then touched the glass gently, as if it might burn her. "We were so young. So young."

I watched her drift back in her mind. "Angelique was always the baby. She was only a year younger, but Mama always called her Baby." She tilted the picture toward me and whispered, "Wasn't she beautiful?"

I nodded. "You both were."

She gave me a sad little smile, then lay back against the pillow and closed her eyes. A little stream of tears started running across her temples, and before you know it, she was sobbing again. Finally she wiped her eyes and looked at me. "I was such a fool."

Now, I knew she wasn't talking about all the times she'd chased me down the hall or the way she'd trapped me coming up the fire escape stairs, or even the phone calls she'd made about me to the manager. It was like none of that had ever happened. She was talking about something big. Something that had made the Daisy then into the Daisy now.

Very gently I asked, "Did it have to do with Angelique?"

She looked at the picture and nodded.

"Do you want me to call her?"

She shook her head. "She's gone off to be with Mama." She touched the picture again and sighed. "And Billy McCabe."

"Who?"

She sat up a bit. "Billy McCabe. He was a boy in my class. He asked me out for malts and I went, even though I didn't particularly like him. When he brought me home, he took one look at Angelique and that was it. They were in love."

"But if you didn't particularly like him..."

She choked out a laugh and said, "I thought that she should've found someone in her own class. But what I thought didn't matter a hoot to her. She went off and became Mrs. Billy McCabe. And while she was picking out china and linens, I was working in a factory canning apricots. And the more those rotten yellow things came rollin' down the belt, the more I started hating Angelique.

"She was always writing me, telling me that I'd find somebody someday and be as happy as she was. And I could tell that she really wanted me to so she wouldn't have to feel guilty anymore about stealing Billy from me."

"But—"

"So I decided I *wouldn't* find someone. Why on earth would I find someone just to make Angelique happy? Suitors would call, and Mama would tell me to go out with them, but I wouldn't. I'd sit down and write Angelique a letter instead. I wasn't about to let her off the hook for what she'd done.

"Well, one day I turned around and I was thirty, and suitors weren't knocking anymore. Shortly after that Mama died, and after we buried her I only heard from Angelique on my birthday and at Christmas. And then it was usually just chitchat about the weather." She looked back at the picture. "She got Billy and I got nobody."

"But...what about *Mr.* Graybill?"

She shook her head and sighed. "There is no Mr. Graybill. Never has been. You get to an age where everybody assumes you're married and they start calling you Mrs. even if it's supposed to be Miss. It's not the kind of thing you want to constantly go and correct people on." She looked at me. "My name's Daisy Lorraine Graybill. Always has been, always will be."

Well, let me tell you, I had shivers running all through me. Creepy, scary shivers. And I think she saw me shudder, because her lips tried to crack into a smile as she said, "I know what you're thinking, Samantha, and you're right. But there's nothing I can do about it now." She put out her hand for me to hold. It felt rough and cold. "All these years I thought I was justified. All these years I blamed every misfortune on her." She closed her eyes and then, from deep inside her throat she whispered, "I'm sorry, Angelique. I was such a fool."

I sat there, frozen, not wanting to pull my hand away but not wanting to leave it there, either. In a little while her grip loosened and a bit of drool ran out of the corner of her mouth. I whispered, "Mrs. Graybill?" She didn't answer, so I slipped my hand free and tiptoed out of there.

And it's not that I was in a hurry to get to the Landvogt

mansion. I wasn't even thinking about Mrs. Landvogt. I was thinking about Mrs. Graybill and her sister and Billy McCabe. And for some reason I started running. Hard. And I kept right on running—down the road, across the street, past the supermarket—as fast as I could. And the whole time I was running I was checking back over my shoulder at the nursing home. Like I was running from something that was chasing me.

Something that would kill me if it could catch me.

ELEVEN

I thought Tina was going to fall down and kiss my feet. "Oh, thank God you're here! Mother's beside herself." She let me in and the alarm *bo-beep*ed as she closed the door behind me.

I asked, "Is that thing *always* on?"

"The Tattler? Twenty-four hours a day." She gave me a wry little smile. "Mother began her paranoia phase when I went away to college." She did a double take at the Christmas tree. "Oh, look at that," she said, then switched the lights on. "It's dismal enough around here without forgetting to turn on the tree."

"Went away to college? But I thought you lived at home."

She laughed. "Yeah, I guess so," and then added, "That's been temporary for about a year now."

I guess I still looked puzzled, because she leaned in and whispered, "I'm a disgraceful dropout." She led me toward the kitchen, saying, "Mother's managed to spread her stuff out over the entire top floor, so I've been sequestered to the servants' quarters." She scowled and said, "Which under the circumstances seems apt, don't you think?"

I didn't even want to touch that, so I just followed her into the kitchen and watched as she put a glass of water on a little silver tray. She shook her head and said, "Personally, I think Mother should ask her doctor for a sedative. Of course, I also think she should tell this friend she has on the police force about Marique, but she won't do *that* either." She rolled her eyes and smirked. "You can see that what I think doesn't count for much around here."

I was following her out of the kitchen when she said, "Oh!" and turned back around.

"What's the matter?"

"If I don't want this thrown in my face," she said with a frown, "I'd better do it right." She put down the tray and said, "Right there in the pantry...could you get me a lemon?"

The pantry was like a walk-in closet for caviar. There were fish eggs and fish eyes, pickled eel and smoked partridge. I moved over an aisle and saw grape leaves, gingered garlic, ostrich paté, candied rhubarb, and then a whole bunch of stuff I couldn't even pronounce.

I was trying to keep my brain on lemons, but I'd never seen food like that before. And I guess I got sidetracked, because when Tina called, "On the bottom shelf in the back!" I jumped like I'd been caught snitching cookie dough.

I found the lemons all right, and I probably would've rushed one right out to her, only this small panel of switches and lights on the wall caught my eye. And I was trying to figure out what in the world it was, when Tina popped her head in and said, "Did you get lost?"

I gave her the lemon and pointed to the panel. "What *is* that?"

"The Panel of Paranoia," she said with a laugh. "You know—the security panel."

I smiled back at her and said a real profound "Oh."

We moved back into the kitchen, where she cut a very thin slice out of the center of the lemon and slid it into the water. She repositioned a napkin, gave me a little smile, and said, "Ready?"

We both kind of studied the chandelier on the ride upstairs. Halfway up, I asked, "So it's just the two of you living here?"

"What do you mean?"

I shrugged. "I guess I was expecting cooks and maids and gardeners and stuff."

She laughed. "You're looking at 'em."

"You do all that?"

"Well, not all of it. And we did used to have help but…I don't know. Mother'd get mad and fire one and then she wouldn't replace them. She still calls in a cleaning lady every once in a while, but when I moved back I got saddled with the day-to-day stuff."

When the elevator came to a stop, she pushed the door open and whispered, "I wish she wasn't doing this to you. You seem really nice."

I felt like telling her the same thing, but I didn't—we were already at the Crocodile's door. Tina peeked inside. "Mother?" She came back out and headed farther down the hallway. "She must've gone into her office."

We stopped at the last doorway before the hallway turned. Tina knocked on the open door. "Mother?"

"Bring her in!"

She'd been dipped in lavender. Silky, shiny lavender. But the minute she turned from her desk I knew—she was definitely still a crocodile. She looked at her watch. "You're almost an hour late."

I knew there was no sense telling her about Mrs. Graybill. "I'm sorry."

Tina put the tray down near her mother and asked, "Is there anything else I can get you?"

"Some privacy would be nice."

The doorbell rang. Tina sighed and said, "I'll get that," and disappeared.

Mrs. Landvogt zoomed her wheelchair straight at me and said, "Sit down. I want to know what you've got. Every last detail. I want to know where you've been, who you've talked to, and what they've said—everything."

She practically ran me into an ironwood chair with dragonhead arms. I tried stalling. "What about that phone call you got?"

"What about it?"

"Did you tape it?"

"Tape it…no! How am I supposed to tape it?"

"Don't you have an answering machine?"

"Of course I have an answering machine!"

"Where is it?"

She pointed to her desk. "Over there. You mean to tell me I can record a conversation with that thing?"

I felt like crossing my eyes at her. "It's a recorder…?"

"So how do I do that?" she snapped.

I went over to her desk and opened the tape panel. "Right here: 'To Record a Telephone Conversation: Tap MEMO/2WAY.'"

The Croc zoomed over and looked down the bridge of

her nose at the instructions. "Well, why didn't you tell me that before? I could've had his voice on tape!"

I closed my eyes and tried to count to ten. "So it was a man?"

"That's right."

The security system *be-boop*ed in the distance. "What did he sound like? Any accent?"

"He sounded mechanical. Like he was holding his nose."

"Well, what did he say exactly? What does he want to do? An exchange?"

She hacked out a laugh. "That's right. This Friday night at eight o'clock, under the clock in the mall." She knocked on her cast. "Tell me how I'm supposed to deliver that kind of money in this condition?"

"Mrs. Landvogt, why don't you call the police? Tina says you have a friend there who—"

"Don't start with that again! You know what they'll do to her." She scowled and added, "Besides, Andy would botch the whole thing. He can't find his way out of a paper sack."

"But the mall, the Friday night before Christmas...he'll just disappear into the crowds."

She buffed a thumbnail, saying, "That scenario is really irrelevant because we both know you'll find her before then."

"But—"

She put her hand out before her, admiring her claws. "You've proved it already."

"I haven't done anything!"

"Sure you have. The way you tricked me into telling you about Royce, that bit with the recorder. You're clever, you're resourceful, and you're motivated." She looked straight at me. "Aren't you, Samantha?"

There was a knock at the door. The Croc let out an impatient sigh and said under her breath, "That girl will *never* learn to follow directions." She called, "What is it?"

Tina came in with a cardboard box. "I'm sorry, Mother, but I'm worried. It was just like when the ransom note was left."

The Croc froze. "What do you mean?"

"There was no one there. I checked all the way down to the street. I didn't see a soul. Just this on the porch."

"Well, open it!"

Tina tore off the tape but then hesitated and handed the box over to her mother. "Here...maybe you should."

The Croc pulled back one flap, then the other, then screamed. Like she'd opened a box of tarantulas.

I took a step closer and right away I knew that the special delivery didn't contain flowers. I put my hand in the box and came up with a fistful of fur. Orange fur.

I didn't know crocodiles could faint. But this one did, right there in her chair.

Tina rushed over to her mother and fanned her with an envelope while I checked the box. It was Marique all right. Her tags, her fur—everything but her body.

When the Croc came to she whispered, "Is she...is she...?"

I picked up some fur and said, "Yup. She's bald."

"She's...what?"

"Bald. It's all fur."

The Croc picked up the box and whispered, "Maaaar-iiique!" Then she said it again, only louder, "Maaaariiique!"

Now, there was something about the way she said her dog's name that made my back tingle. But it wasn't until she said it *again* that it hit me—hers was the voice I had heard the night of the parade.

I looked at her, crying over a box full of fuzz, and realized—I didn't have a clue what was going on here. Not a clue.

* * *

It was dark by the time I got away from the Landvogt mansion. And maybe I should've gone straight home, but I was dying to tell Marissa about the fur bomb and besides, I was thirsty and there's always a shelf full of sodas in the McKenzes' refrigerator.

Marissa's eyes bugged right out when she saw me. She yanked me in by the arm and said, "Sammy! Oh my God, why didn't you tell me?"

"Tell you?"

"About your mom!"

A big uh-oh stuck in my throat. "What about my mom?"

"That's her, isn't it? On TV?"

I sat down in a chair and hid my face behind my hands. "Oh, no!"

"What's the matter? I thought she wanted to be on TV."

I looked at her through my fingers. "As the GasAway Lady?"

She laughed. "Well it's a start, right?"

"You sound just like Grams. That stupid commercial is more like *Boom!* The End. I mean, who's going to want to put the Amazing Expanding Woman in a movie? It's embarrassing!"

Marissa shrugged. "It's not that bad…Even Mom thought it was pretty good."

"Your mother saw it?"

Marissa nodded, then hitched a thumb toward the kitchen. "She's actually in there cooking dinner."

"*Cooking* cooking?"

She rolled her eyes. "Yeah. She and Dad joined some gourmet club and I think we're her guinea pigs. C'mon. She's even wearing an apron."

I followed her and laughed. "This I've got to see…!"

Mrs. McKenze looked over from her six-burner stove with a smile. "Hello, Sammy. What a pleasant surprise. Can you stay for supper? We're having"—she checked her cookbook—"*costolette di vitello alla milanese.*"

Marissa whispered, "Veal cutlets."

Well, it did smell good, but from looking at the set table I could tell I'd never be able to figure out which fork went with which part of the dinner. And between silverware etiquette and polite conversation about the GasAway Lady, I figured that I wouldn't be able to eat much.

I smiled at her and said, "No, but thanks. Grams is expecting me." Then I remembered that Marissa had said that her mom had met the Crocodile once, so I asked, "Mrs. McKenze? What do you know about Lilia Landvogt?"

She poured some olive oil into a frying pan. "Not

much, really. I was over at her house one time for a dinner party, but she didn't really impress me as someone I wanted to get to know."

"Why not?"

"Oh, I don't know." She played with the flame under the pan. "I think it was mostly the comments she made about her daughter."

"About Tina?"

"She was mad at her, and I could even understand why. I just don't think it's appropriate to talk ill of your children in public like that."

"What was she doing? Calling her names or something?"

Mrs. McKenze peeled a piece of breaded veal off a plate and slid it into the oil. "I don't even remember. I just came away thinking that she was not a very nice woman."

"How long ago was this?"

Another piece of veal sizzled into the oil. "Oh, it's been years. Years and years." She turned the flame down a bit. "Why all the questions, Sammy?"

I looked down. "She's...uh...kind of mad at me."

"Lilia is?"

I nodded.

"In heaven's name why?"

I eyed Marissa, who just shrugged and shook her head, so I said, "To make a long story short, I was in charge of her dog and it ran away."

For a second there I thought Mrs. McKenze was going to drop the veal. "Well, then you know exactly what I mean."

"I *do?*"

"Sure. That's the same reason she was mad at Tina!"

All of a sudden I felt dizzy. "Wait a minute—*Tina* lost their dog?"

"That's right. Lilia said she left the gate open and it ran away."

"Was it a Pomeranian?"

"I don't even know, to tell you the truth."

"Was it named Marique?"

She flipped the veal over in the frying pan. "Is that the name of the dog you were taking care of?"

I nodded.

"Well, then it couldn't have been. The dog I'm talking about was found a few blocks down Jasmine." She wiped her hands on a dishtowel. "It had been run over by a car."

TWELVE

I couldn't go straight home. Not with everything I had swimming around in my brain. I mean, talking the whole thing over with Marissa helped some, but I was miles from a solution. Miles and miles.

So I went to Hudson's. And I don't think I went there to actually *talk* to him. I just wanted to kind of sit around on his porch and wait for things to make sense to me.

Trouble is, Hudson wasn't on the porch. He was in the house. Cooking. And as I followed him back to the kitchen I knew right away—he wasn't making *costolette di vitello alla milanese*. He was making waffles.

He popped a plate out of the drainer and put it next to another, already waiting on the counter. "Why don't you call your grandmother—tell her you're staying for supper." He grinned at me. "Or dessert, if that's how you fancy dressing your waffle."

He didn't have to ask me twice. I called Grams, and before you know it I was sitting down at Hudson's table pouring syrup on my waffle.

Hudson put a fried egg on his. He smeared the yolk around and then put a slice of ham on top and poured syrup over the whole mess. He grinned like a five-year-old. "Nothing quite like it in the whole wide world."

I laughed. "What is it?"

He took a great big bite. "Delicious."

So I had my dinner-dessert and he had his mega-mess, and our tummies were both happy by the time the batter ran out. I was helping clear the table when he asked, "So how are things with Elyssa?"

"Great! I've been taking her over to the nursing home where her mother works after school. She tells me stories about her teacher and this troublemaker kid named Shane—she's really funny."

He grinned at me. "Imagine that." He sprayed up some suds in the sink and asked, "And Heather? Any progress there?"

So I told him what I'd been doing at school and how Heather was acting so nervous, and when I got to the part about Kris Kringles and how she'd thrown away her cupcake, he laughed and said, "This is perfect!"

I shrugged. "I can't see her actually confessing."

"Don't underestimate the power of a guilty mind."

He scrubbed dishes and I dried, and when we were about done he microwaved some cocoa and said, "What about the rest of your life? You still don't want to talk about it?"

I just sighed. "I can't, Hudson."

We went onto the porch and sat there, looking at the sky. The stars were out and there was a little cloud like a feather pillow moving across the bottom of the moon. Finally Hudson said, "You're afraid I'll tell your grandmother, aren't you?"

I just watched the cloud puff along the moon.

"Have I ever done that in the past?"

I shook my head a little.

"Sometimes it helps to let these things out."

I wanted to tell him. All about Mrs. Landvogt and the way she was blackmailing me. All about Paula Nook and Mr. Petersen and Hero, the Preposterous Peeing Machine. But what came out of my mouth was, "You know Mrs. Graybill?"

"That meddlesome woman down the hall?"

I nodded. "She's in a nursing home."

He studied me for a minute, then looked up at the sky. "I wouldn't wish a nursing home on anyone." He smoothed back an eyebrow and said, "In your case, though, it doesn't seem to be providing the relief that one might expect."

I let out a big sigh, then told him about how she'd acted like I was a long-lost friend, wanting to hold my hand and stuff. And when I got to the part about Billy McCabe and her sister, he shook his head and said, "That's a shame. Worse, that's a waste. From the outside it seems so senseless, but from inside, spite is like an addiction. Like greed or power. It's certainly as strong a motivator." He cupped his cocoa in his hands and blew on the steam. "The cure's a little forgiveness, but it seems hard to come by for some." He turned to me. "She has no one?"

I looked back up at the moon and shook my head. No one, I thought.

No one but me.

* * *

I was on my way home to Grams when I got an idea. A very bad idea. Now, there's no way I look anything but underage, but the more I thought about it, the more I rationalized that Palmer's was a bar and *grill*, not just a bar, and that maybe—just maybe—there was an area of video games where I could hole up and spy on Paula Nook.

Palmer's is out on West Main. Not quite as far as Petersen's Prints, but almost. And I don't really know what I was going there to watch Paula do; it just seemed more constructive than sitting around the Senior Highrise wishing for an answer.

Now, I wasn't really thinking about Mr. Petersen—he was like a block away in my mind. But as I walked past the parking lot I did a double take, because sitting right there between an old Toyota and a lowered four-by-four was his Bug on Wheels.

That got me a little nervous. I mean, Paula Nook might not really remember me. Not if she looked at me with both eyes, anyway. But Mr. Petersen? That was another story.

So I stood there in the parking lot, watching the martini glass in the Palmer's sign flicker, telling myself that I should go home. I really should go home. But finally I decided that it couldn't hurt to check things out a little.

I peered in the front door but couldn't see much past an entry wall, so I went back around the corner, past the Bugmobile, and crouched behind a garbage can that was propping open a side door. Inside were two men working in the kitchen; one was rinsing down the sink, and the other was smashing the grease out of a patty on the grill. There were boxes all over the floor—like someone had been stocking up on paper towels and onions—and right in front of the refrigerator was a rolling rack of hamburger buns and bread. There wasn't a copper pan in sight.

109

Next to the grill, on a back burner, was a big pot of soup that was bubbling and spurting like lava from a volcano. The guy at the sink yelled something in Spanish to the guy at the grill, who reached over and turned the heat down.

So there I am, cuddled up to a garbage can, holding as still as I can, when what comes crawling across my feet? A rat. And I'm not talking mouse, here—I'm talking this thing could eat cats.

I banged the trash can pretty good trying to get away from it, and when the goulash gourmets looked over to see what was causing all the commotion, well, I didn't wait for them to chase me down. I just scrambled around the corner and hid in the back alley.

The alley was a trash heap. I kept one eye out for monster mice while I watched for the cooks to appear at the kitchen door. When they didn't show, I took a look down the alley and noticed that Palmer's back door was propped open, too.

I worked my way through the garbage to the back door and peeked inside. There was a skinny hallway that ramped up to some pool tables at the back of the restaurant. On one side of it were more boxes; on the other, two bathrooms. The Women's room door was shut, with an Out of Order sign posted on it, but the Men's door was wide open. And I'm sure that it was functional and all, but, well, let's just say that if Hero was walking by, even *he* wouldn't have stopped.

I didn't want to stand there all night checking out boxes and bathrooms, so I finally headed up the ramp into the cloud of cigarette smoke.

When I got to the pool tables I ducked around the corner and tried to disappear in a chair in the shadows. There was a lady wearing an Indiana Jones hat and a kind of gypsy dress with a lot of blouse buttons missing. She was playing pool against this guy with a Fu Manchu mustache and a shaved head, and I think she was winning, because while she was sashaying around the table chalking her cue stick and taking shots, he stood back looking pretty mad.

Now, what I should've been doing was looking over the divider for Paula Nook or Mr. Petersen, but I couldn't seem to keep my eyes off the Gypsy. She had roses tattooed on her legs, and had on sandals that weren't really sandals at all. They had no soles. Just a long strap of leather looped around the second toe and then wrapped up around the ankle and tied in front. And she was kind of large, but the way she moved was really graceful. Like she was doing a tango with the table.

When she sinks the last ball, she says, "Nice game" to Fu Manchu. He grumbles something about snakes in the grass, then slaps a twenty-dollar bill on the table and disappears.

She stuffs the twenty inside her gypsy dress, then chalks up Fu's stick and says, "You any good?"

She had her back to me, so I didn't think she was talking to me, and I just sat there in the dark, looking around for who she *was* talking to.

She turns around and hands me the stick. "Don't be shy. Get up here."

I whisper, "I...I can't. I'm sorry. I was just watching."

She squints through the smoke at me. "Ooh, you *are* young."

"Shhh!"

She grabs her bottle of beer, sits down next to me, and whispers, "We hiding from someone?"

I shook my head.

"Then come on! No one's gonna care. Not if you're not drinkin'."

"I can't. I—"

She grabbed me by the arm and said, "Oh, come on. It'll be fun. I'll teach ya."

Now, I didn't want to learn. I just wanted to hide in my corner and look for the Cyclops and the Stinkbug. But she was getting pretty loud, and I was afraid that if I kept arguing I'd get thrown out before I had a chance to see anything.

She put the cue stick in my hand, then leaned onto the pool table with her own. "You right-handed?"

I nodded.

"Good. Right here now, next to me. Hold it like this with your right hand. Prop it like this on your left hand... Come on now, what are you looking at over there?"

"Oh, sorry." I tried to copy what she was doing, but it felt really awkward. Like the handle was too big and the tip was too small and there was about a mile of wood in between the two.

"Okay, now slide it back and forth...no, no, *easy*... there you go."

So there I am, learning to tango with a pool table, when I notice Paula Nook walk by with a tray of food.

The Gypsy watches me watching her. "You know Paula?"

"Uh, no."

She laughs. "You're a terrible liar."

I felt like dropping my stick and running. I mean, what was I going to find out there anyway? No one was going to talk to a thirteen-year-old. Not one who was stupid enough to walk into Palmer's after dark, anyway.

She held on to my arm and said, "Hey, hey, chill. Come on over here," then sat me back down in the corner. "I really thought you'd have fun. Thought you were just being shy." She looked right at me and whispered, "What's got you so amped?"

I checked over my shoulder at the dining tables and then did a double take. Paula Nook had delivered the order to Mr. Petersen, only she hadn't just left it there. She'd sat down across from him.

The Gypsy said, "It's Paula, isn't it?"

I decided not to answer her. "Do you know the guy she's with?"

"Royce? Sure. He's a regular."

"Are they friends?"

"Him and Paula? I guess so. Not *friend* friends, if that's what you mean. More like business acquaintances."

Now, Mr. Petersen and Paula Nook weren't sitting at that table discussing the weather. She was huddled up across from him, jabbing her finger in the air like she was trying to convince him that the world was round. He sat there shaking his head like he knew darned well it was flat, and no matter what she said, it was going to stay flat.

The Gypsy said, "Well, dust my chalk. I've never seen her act like *that* around him before." She scratched up and down one of her rose tattoos and mumbled, "Me and Paula have gotta have a little talk if she's tanglin' with him."

113

"Wait. No! Why?"

Her eyelids came in for a landing. "You some kind of narc for the wife?"

"No! I'm just...I'm just trying to get out of this gigantic mess I'm in."

"Yeah?" Her eyes opened back up. "Anything I can do to help?"

I shook my head. "Just don't let them know I was—" Then Mr. Petersen looks up, straight at me. I gulp, "Here."

For a minute he just stares. Then he taps Paula on the arm and points at me.

Well, I guess she did recognize me, even with both eyes, because she was up in a flash, charging after me.

I said, "Gotta go!" to the Gypsy and flew down the ramp to the back door like a cannonball. And I would've hit the alley and hurdled rhino rats all the way back to the street, only as I ran by the women's bathroom I heard something. Something high and yippy.

The Cyclops was charging down the ramp after me, but I did a U-turn anyway and yanked on the Women's door-knob. It didn't budge.

Now, I've never been thrown out of a place before. Not literally, anyway. But all of a sudden the Cyclops is clamping on to my sweatshirt and jeans, saying, "If ya gotta pee...use the bushes," as she's heaving me into the alley.

The door slams shut, and there I am, in the dirt, in the dark, only a few yards away from what's probably my way out of the Crocodile's jaws, and there's only one thing on my mind.

Getting back inside.

THIRTEEN

It didn't take me long to get up. If that really was Marique yipping in the women's bathroom, I had to break the door down. That, or call the police and tell them there was a bomb in the building. Or children being tortured in the bathroom. *Some*thing.

The back door was locked up tight, and since the rats hadn't exactly had a pay phone installed in the alley for my convenience, I went around the building to the kitchen door. Somebody had closed it, too. So I was on my way to tackle Palmer's from the front, when who should come storming out? Big Bug Petersen.

He was on the lookout for me, all right, he just wasn't looking in the right spot. He checked up and down Main Street, and then, while he's jingling around trying to find the right key to the Bugmobile, he turns around and practically steps on me.

He backpedaled a bit, saying, "Get away from me! I got nothin' to say to you!"

I just stood there, looking straight at him.

"I'm serious!"

He skittered past me, and from the way he was acting, I knew he was guilty of something. And watching him shaking the key into his Bug on Wheels it hit me that he wasn't just trying to hide something from me—he was desperate about something.

I took a stab and said, "If you lose your business, that doesn't leave you with much, does it, Mr. Petersen?"

He plopped in his car and slammed the door.

I called through the window, "'Course, fifty grand might help out a bit...if you could get it."

The window zoomed down and all of a sudden I was looking down the barrel of his handgun again. "If I've told you this once, I've told you a hundred times—stay out of it!"

Now, you may think at this point I'd be getting used to him poking a gun in my face, but let me tell you, I wasn't. I jumped back, threw my hands up, and then stood there all bug-eyed as he squealed out of the parking lot. And I was in the middle of remembering how people turn up dead on the west side all the time when I heard, "That was not cool."

I spun around, and there was the Gypsy looking really disgusted. She took a couple of steps closer saying, "Hey, don't freak. He's gone."

All of a sudden my legs felt wobbly and I couldn't seem to breathe right. I sat down on a parking curb and held my head in my hands, and before I could stop myself, I was crying.

She sat down next to me, and for the longest time she didn't say a word. Finally she whispered, "I think you're in way over your head."

I wiped the tears off my face and laughed, "You can say that again."

"So get out."

"I can't!"

"Why not?"

I almost told her. Everything. But what came out of my mouth instead was, "I've got to get into that bathroom!"

"The bathroom?" She gave me a funny look and said, "Just go in the alley. I'll keep an eye out."

I shook my head. "I've got to get that dog."

She reached over and touched my forehead. "What dog?"

"The one in the ladies' room."

"There's no dog in there."

"How do you know?"

"I was just in there."

"But it's out of order!"

"I didn't use it. I peed in the men's, but they don't have a mirror, so I went into the ladies'."

"But it was locked!"

She studied me a minute. "I think maybe you should go home and have some warm milk."

"It...it wasn't locked?"

She shook her head. "I walked right in."

"And there wasn't a dog inside?"

"No..." She stopped and looked at me. "Come to think of it, though, there was a water dish on the floor."

I jumped up and said, "I knew it!"

"Whoa, whoa! Down, girl! In the first place, you don't want to go barging back in there. It's obvious Royce wasn't wild about you sniffing around his watering hole, and to tell you the truth, I don't think I've ever seen anything throw Paula the way you did. Certainly not a kid."

"You don't understand...!"

"And I don't hear you explaining."

We stared at each other a minute, and then I told her. All about the dog. All about being blackmailed. All about everything. And when I finally came up for air, her eyebrows had about disappeared into her hat. "You on the level?"

I threw my hands in the air. "What do you think? I go around getting guns shoved up my nose for fun?"

"Chill! I'm sorry! It's just that...wow." She tapped a finger against her lips, then said, "Paula's got a dog."

"Yeah, I know. Ribs. Does she bring him to work?"

"I've only seen him a couple of times and then she's shooed him back in the kitchen."

"When's the last time you saw him?"

She shrugged and said, "I don't know...Maybe a week ago?" She retied the strap of a sandal. "What kind of dog is it you're looking for?"

"A Pomeranian."

She laughed, "Hers ain't no Pomeranian. Basically, it's got no hair."

"Neither does this one."

"What?"

So I explained to her about the fur bomb and said, "I used to know what she looked like, but now I haven't got a clue. She probably looks more like a rat than a dog."

The Gypsy laughed, then got up and said, "You know what? I'm going back in there to have a look-see. If I spot any oversized rats I'll let you know." She looked over her shoulder at me. "Get over here out of the light, would you? This ain't the best place for you to be hanging out."

So I moved into the shadows and waited. And a few minutes later the Gypsy came back saying, "I guess Paula took off for the night. Desi says she said something about an emergency and split. I checked the kitchen—no rats there. Other than the regulars, of course. I checked the bathroom, too. No rats, but there is a water bowl."

"Is there water in it?"

She nodded. "I'd tell you to sneak a peek yourself, but I think you'd live longer if you went home."

I thought about it and agreed. If Marique had been in the bathroom, she was gone now, and there wasn't any reason to go back inside. So I tell her thanks, and I'm heading up to the sidewalk when she calls, "Hey! What if I hear something? How do I get ahold of you?"

Now, she seemed nice and everything, but I didn't think I ought to give a pool shark with rose tattoos and soleless sandals my grams' number, if you know what I mean. But then I didn't want to miss out if she heard something, either. Finally I said, "I go to William Rose Junior High. It lets out a little after three."

"Got it," she said, then disappeared into the shadows.

FOURTEEN

Heather didn't even rattle the box on her desk. She just pitched it into the trash and tried to avoid my evil eye.

Me, I got another pasta present. This time it was a snowflake made out of macaroni. And actually, it was amazing. It was painted white and sprinkled with glittery blue and white specks. I peeked over at Monique, but she wasn't looking at me at all. Neither was Brandy or Tawnee. And I couldn't tell about Cassie—there was too much hair in the way. I check around for other prospects, but when Marissa flashed me her Polaroid camera, I forgot all about Kris Kringles and started thinking about our plan.

When homeroom was over, Marissa, Holly, and I huddled up in a corner, and I got a little lesson in how to point and shoot. Marissa handed it to me and said, "Happy hunting."

I went hunting, all right. Trouble was, I couldn't find the Beast. Not between homeroom and first period. Not between first and second. Not between second and third. And I was starting to worry that she really was going to pull off sneaking by me between classes when I spotted her ducking into Miss Pilson's classroom.

I did a U-turn and popped in behind her.

She takes one look at me and says, "This isn't your class-room, get out!"

I held the camera up to my eye and moved in.

"What are you doing? Get away from me!"

I pressed the button. The camera sputtered and whined, and spat out a picture.

"Hey, you can't do that! Give that here!"

What I gave her was my best I'm-gonna-get-you stare, and I ducked out the door.

At lunch I zipped into the library and got two more. The first one came out great, but she hid her face behind a book when I took the second one, so I tossed it.

After school I got one of her coming down the steps, and when she saw me wagging the picture she blocked her face from me with a notebook and ran off.

I tucked the pictures away and smiled as I headed off to pick up Elyssa. If Officer Borsch couldn't pick Heather out of a crowd after seeing those, he was the world's biggest mole.

Elyssa didn't waste time saying hello. She raced down the steps and said, "You're never going to believe this. He flooded the classroom!"

"Who, Shane?"

"Yeah! He plugged up the sink with gum and turned the water on when we went out for lunch. When we came back, Miss Ugalde slipped and fell and got her rear end all soaked."

"Did she get hurt?"

"She got mad!" Elyssa giggled. "It looked like she wet her pants!"

She skipped along beside me, going on and on about Miss Ugalde and Shane, but when we got to Cook Street and I said, "I've got to stop off at the police station for a minute, okay?" she got real quiet.

"Why do we have to go over there?"

"I have to talk to Officer Borsch."

She stopped walking and crossed her arms. "I hate him."

I laughed. "I know. Me too."

"So why do we have to go visit him?"

I thought about this a minute. Then I pulled out the pictures of Heather and said, "See her?"

"Yeah?"

"She's my Shane."

Elyssa looked through the pictures and said, "I think I saw her at the Christmas parade."

"You did? Where?"

"Just walking by. I saw her when we were getting ready."

"Are you sure?"

She laughed and nodded. "I thought she was a clown."

I looked at the pictures again, and it hit me how I was so used to the way Heather looked that I didn't really *see* her anymore. But with her wild red hair and earlobes loaded with jewelry, she did look like a clown. A kind of crabby clown, but a clown.

"Was she wearing any kind of costume?"

"Nuh-uh."

"Did she have a cat?"

"A *cat*? Nuh-uh. At least I don't think so. I just saw her walking by when we were getting ready." All of a sudden her hands flew up to her mouth. "Do you think *she's* the one who threw the cats?"

I nodded. "Which is why I want to go to the police station, okay?"

She didn't say yes, but she didn't say no, either. We walked along, and when we got to the station, she sat down on a bench right outside the door and said, "Hurry, okay?"

"Why don't you come in with me?"

She shook her head.

I pulled open the door. "Please?"

She crossed her arms and stuck out her bottom lip. "No."

I looked inside and then back at her. "Okay. You wait right here. I'll be quick."

The lady at the counter was wearing a uniform with patches and all, but she still looked more like she should be serving rat burgers at Palmer's than working for the police. Her hair was bleached but was poking out black roots everywhere, and her orange fingernail polish had been chipped about halfway back. She was digging through some papers on the counter, and with her hair and her nails and her humongous nose she looked like a giant bird with a nest on its head, scratching for grubs.

She looked up at me. "Yes...?"

"I'm...I'm looking for Officer Borsch."

She scratched through her nest, saying, "He's off today. Is there something I can help you with?"

I glanced over my shoulder at Elyssa sitting on the bench. "No, I'll just stop by tomorrow."

"Do you want to leave a message?"

I started for the door. "No...well, maybe you can tell him I'll come back tomorrow. About this time."

"And you are...?"

"Sammy. Tell him it's about the cats."

She raised her beak a few inches. "Oh, the *cats*. He'll want to hear about that."

It sounded like she was making fun of me, and I almost said something back to her, but I didn't. I figured anyone who went through life looking like a vagrant dodo didn't really understand how they came across anyway.

I went outside and said, "Ready?" to Elyssa.

She didn't stand up. "If I had to choose between Shane and Gil, I'd choose Shane."

I stood there looking at her until it hit me what she was getting at. I sat down next to her and said, "I don't like Officer Borsch any more than you do, but I also don't think Heather's funny like you think Shane is. She's just plain mean." I stood up and put out my hand. "Ol' Borsch-head may be grumpy and fat and ugly, but he doesn't go out and *try* to hurt people like Heather does." She took my hand and we started down the walkway. "Don't get me wrong, it's not an easy call, but I'm in a big mess and it's partly because of Heather."

"Because of the cats?"

"Let's just say that if Heather is the one who let those cats go, she's made my life a lot more complicated than it would've been if she *hadn't* let them go."

"Why?"

So I started talking about Mrs. Landvogt and what a crocodile she was, and for some reason I began talking like her and pretending I *was* her. And since it made Elyssa laugh, I started really getting into it, and I guess I

124

got carried away because all of a sudden she stops laughing and says, "She said that?"

It took me a minute to switch from being the Crocodile. "Said what?"

"That she'd throw you out in the street if you didn't find her dog?"

I tried to backpedal in a hurry. I mean, her mom *was* friends with Officer Borsch, and the last thing I needed was for him to find out what I'd said.

She could tell I was trying to cover up, though. She tugged on my arm and whispered, "I'm not gonna tell!"

I knew she could keep a secret—I mean, that was why I was walking her home in the first place—but I was still feeling pretty stupid for getting so carried away in front of her.

When we arrived at the nursing home, the first thing the receptionist did was call down the hall, "She's here!"

At first I thought Mrs. Keltner was worried because I was a little late bringing her daughter in, but when she came around the corner I realized it didn't have a thing to do with Elyssa. She said to me, "I'm glad you're here. Daisy's been asking for you all day."

I followed her down the hall. "She's been asking for me?"

"More like demanding. I thought she was going to blow a gasket when I told her I wouldn't pull you out of school so you could visit her."

When we got close to her room I could hear, "Samaaaan-thaaaaa...Samaaaanthaaaaa...Samaaaanthaaaaa," coming down the hallway like the voice of a ghost. Shivers ran all through me and I had to just stop and listen a minute.

"Samaaaanthaaaaa…Samaaaanthaaaaa…Samaaaanthaaaaa…"
came her voice, over and over again.

Mrs. Keltner whispered, "She's been doing that all day.
Every waking moment. She wouldn't even touch her lunch."

I tiptoed into the room and sat down in the chair beside
her bed. She was wrapped up in her robe with her eyes
closed, looking very pale. I whispered, "Mrs. Graybill?"

She said my name a few more times, then sputtered to
a stop and opened her eyes—first just a crack, then all the
way. Her eyes were glassy, like they had a film of tears
across them. She let out a sigh. "You're here."

I didn't know what to say. I just scooted around in my
chair a bit and said, "Do you need me to get you something from your apartment?"

Her head moved back and forth against the pillow as
she put out her hand and said it again, "You're here."

Her hand was cold and rough, and holding it felt very
strange. Like holding hands with a statue. She looked into
my eyes and whispered, "Forgive me, Samantha. I'm so
sorry. Please forgive me."

I almost said, Forgive you for what? but then I remembered all the times she'd barged through Grams' apartment
looking for me. The times she'd lain in wait, hoping I'd slip
up so she could kick me out of the Senior Highrise. The
times her hand had practically cut my arm off while she
sprayed threats in my face. What could I say, though? I
looked down, then shrugged and nodded.

She didn't blink. "The truth, Samantha. I need to hear
the truth. Can you forgive me?"

I thought about it seriously this time. About the things

she'd done, about the things she'd said, about the way she'd hated me—it was like looking through little snapshots of my life with her. But the most recent snapshots—the ones of her calling my name and crying over her sister—those showed a whole different Daisy Graybill. So finally I squeezed her hand and whispered, "Of course I forgive you."

She closed her eyes and took a really deep breath, then little by little, she let it out. She mouthed, Thank you, and then closed her eyes.

I watched her, lying there in her dirty pink robe, her chest going up and down, up and down. And I wanted to leave, but somehow I couldn't. I just sat there with my hand in hers, watching her, thinking about the things we'd been through, the things *she'd* been through, and I wondered. About Billy McCabe. About Mrs. Graybill's sister. About her mother. About her life. And somewhere in all that thinking I realized that something about Mrs. Graybill was different. Her hand was still cold, and there was still a drop of drool at the corner of her mouth, but something was different.

Then it hit me. Her chest wasn't going up and down anymore. It was just still. I shook her a little and whispered, "Mrs. Graybill?" Her arm was limp. "Mrs. Graybill!" I stood up and shook her shoulders. "Mrs. Graybill!"

I don't know what happened to me. I'd never felt like that before. Ever. I started shaking and panting for air and running back and forth, trying to figure out what to do. And in the middle of all that, tears started running out of my eyes because I knew—Mrs. Graybill was dead.

I ran into the hallway calling, "Mrs. Keltner! Nurse! *Anybody!*"

Elyssa was right there, sitting on the floor. She jumped up and said, "What's wrong?"

"Mrs. Graybill...she's...she's..."

Elyssa's mom came charging down the hall. She took one look at me and said to Elyssa, "Sit down. Right here. Everything's all right. Just sit."

"But Mom...!"

"Sit!"

Elyssa sat, and her mom and another nurse and I went into the room. They went straight to Mrs. Graybill and checked her out, and it wasn't long before Elyssa's mom was putting her arm around me, whispering, "I'm sorry."

"Is she...is she..."

Mrs. Keltner tried to smile. "She's in a better place now. You've just got to let her go."

I couldn't take it. I stumbled my way down the hall and out the door, and when I got to the curb I sat down and cried. And I cried so hard it almost felt like I had the flu— my stomach was wrenching, my body was shaking, and I couldn't stop. I just couldn't stop.

Then all of a sudden there's a hand on my back and a little voice saying, "I'm sorry she died."

I shook my head.

Elyssa watched me dripping in the gutter a minute, then asked, "Why are you crying? Isn't she in heaven now?"

I slapped some tears away and shook my head. "Who knows where she is. She's *dead*." Then I stood up and said, "I gotta get out of here...." and left her standing there, watching after me.

FIFTEEN

I tried calling Grams from a gas station. The phone must've rung a hundred times before I gave up and stumbled my way over to Hudson's.

He wasn't home, either. And it felt weird, sitting on his porch all by myself, but I was too upset to go anywhere else. At first all I could think of was Mrs. Graybill, but after a while a lady went by trying to power-walk her Pekinese and I remembered: Mrs. Landvogt and Mr. Petersen and Paula Nook. And I felt like saying, Just forget it. It was hopeless. I was never going to get my hands on that blasted bald dog. And really, in the scheme of things, what did it matter anyway?

But thinking about Mrs. Graybill got me crying all over again, so I forced myself to think about the Cyclops. What was she doing with the Stinkbug? And why were they so spooked when they spotted me? It all seemed to come back to the Crocodile. Maybe they were ransoming the dog, or maybe she was blackmailing them. Maybe both. One thing was for sure, it wasn't neither.

So I went back and forth between crying about Mrs. Graybill and fighting to focus on big bugs and Cyclopes and creatures from the swamp. And when my brain was exhausted from its mental tug-of-war, I knew I had to get up and *do* something.

What I decided to do was head back over to Paula Nook's house. I mean, she probably had a gun, too, but I hadn't actually *seen* it yet, so I figured my odds of survival were better than nosing around Petersen's Printing.

So off I went, and when I got to Paula's cul-de-sac, I stood across the road for a few minutes and just watched. There weren't any pickup trucks parked on the street, so at least I was safe from Hero. The curtains were all drawn, and the trash was rolled out to the curb, and even though it was still daylight, the porch light was on. It looked to me like the Cyclops wasn't home.

I went up and banged on the door, and when no one answered I got down on my hands and knees and peeked through the mail slot. All I could really see was dirty tan carpet and the metal legs of two kitchen chairs. I put my mouth up to the slot and called, "Marique! Here, girl!" and then looked inside.

No bald dog ran up to see me.

I tried it again, only this time I called, "Ribs! C'mon, boy!"

Again, no bald dog.

I hurried over to the garage and kind of knocked on the door, whistling and clapping and calling, and I was just about to duck around to the backyard when a scratchy voice came from the house next door, "She took him with her."

I jumped a bit and tried to find the voice, but all I could see were windows with dirty screens over them. It came again. "You some relation?" I wasn't sure, but I thought it was a woman's voice.

"I'm...I'm her niece. She asked me to come over and feed Ribs tonight." I felt like I was lying to a house.

I spotted a window moving further open behind its screen. "Her niece? Paula's never mentioned a niece. 'Course, Paula don't talk much. Especially since that bum Marcus took off."

I forced a laugh and said, "She sure doesn't have much good to say about Marcus anymore."

"No kiddin'! What a piece of work, carryin' on with two other women at the same time. And the way he stiffed her. No alimony, no nothing. Just a piece of that stupid bar across town."

I nodded like I'd heard it all before. Then I tried, "My mom says that Lance guy isn't much better, but I'm hoping he is."

"Oh, I'm afraid your mama's right. Paula's just repeatin' history with that fella. And I tell you what, if his freak dog pisses on my roses one more time I'm gonna hose him down. I got one of them water blasters settin' on my hall table *loaded* with ammonia. I'm just waiting." Then she said, "Oh! There's the timer—gotta go to my brownies!" and slammed the window.

I wasn't about to hang around and wait for the house to start talking again. I peeked over the backyard fence, called for Marique a few times, and then took off. And as I was crossing the road, I looked back over my shoulder and noticed Paula's trash can again, parked on the curb outside her house. And that's when I got the notion that inside that trash can might be some pretty good information. Maybe even evidence.

I ran back, took off the lid, and tried to find something important. Like dog hair or dog food cans—anything. What I found was garbage. Sacks and sacks of stinky garbage. But I started digging through it anyway. And somewhere between black bananas and beer cans I found a soggy ad flyer with a hole cut out of it. Now through my brain flashed Mrs. Landvogt's ransom note, and all of a sudden I knew I was onto something. So I started digging deeper, and pretty soon I had a fist full of smelly flyers with holes cut out of them.

Then all of a sudden something kicked the side of the trash can, *clang!* I popped up, and there she was, as big as a bear, with a pan of brownies in one hand and a water blaster aimed straight at me in the other. She said through a mouthful of chocolate, "I'd wager you're about as related as a bullfrog. What are you after, girl?"

My brain was racing around for a decent lie when out of my mouth pops, "I was just looking for a piece of paper to write her a note...." I started edging away. "Really."

"You're lyin'. I can see it in your eyes." She bit a chunk of brownie right out of the pan.

I held up the ads. "Look! That's what I've got. Paper."

She wagged the blaster at me. "Give 'em here."

"No, I...I..."

"Give 'em here!"

"But I..." I turned around and ran. As fast as I could, as hard as I could.

It wasn't fast enough. She blasted me in the rear end

with ammonia and called, "That's right, girl, *run!* And don't you *ever* come back!"

Believe me, I ran. Clear out to Main Street. And while I was waiting for the light to change I checked out my pants. They were soaked and they *smelled.* I really wanted to get out of them, but when I looked through the flyers I decided that I couldn't just yet. The apartment was one way, the Landvogt mansion was another, and I *had* to see that ransom note.

So I started hiking out to East Jasmine. And somewhere along the way I stopped thinking about brownies and ammonia and started thinking about Mrs. Landvogt. How mean she was, and for what? She had everything.

Then I thought about Mrs. Graybill and Billy McCabe and that whole lifelong disaster, and I felt tired—like my brain was back walking in quicksand, trying to get from one thought to the next.

When I got to the Landvogt mansion, Tina let me in, and the first thing she said when the door had *bo-beep*ed closed was, "What is that *smell?*"

I felt like a sewer rat crashing a party at the White House, but I didn't even care. I looked straight at her. "Ammonia."

"Ammonia?" She wrinkled up her nose. "It smells awful!"

"Yeah, I know." I looked around. "Where's your mom?"

"Watching the stock market." She led me to the den and whispered, "Can I wash those for you or something?"

"I'll make it quick."

The Crocodile's nose was already twitching. She looked over her shoulder and said, "Is that *you* making that stench?"

I took a few steps closer. "Yeah, it's me. I need to see that ransom note."

She fanned the air in front of her. "Oh, that's awful!"

"Look, I got hosed down with ammonia trying to dig up some clues at Paula Nook's house." I held up the ads. "I just want to compare these to the ransom note."

The Croc powered back a few feet. "Hosed down with ammonia?"

"Yeah."

"Paula did that to you?"

"Her neighbor did. Look, I'll get out of here as soon as you show me the note."

She pulled the black book from beside her in the wheelchair and whipped out the ransom note.

My hopes fell the minute I saw it. The note hadn't come from the ads—the letters weren't even close. I muttered, "Rats!"

Tina said softly, "It looks like she was just cutting coupons."

"Then what are these holes?" I handed her a sheet. "No coupon is this size."

"No, but if you're using a box-cutter, you've got to pad, and you wind up with little holes like that."

I looked at her, wondering when on earth Tina Landvogt had ever had to cut coupons. She smiled at me like she'd read my mind. "College. I got pretty good at it."

Just then a noise came out of the Croc like she was being strangled. We both looked at her, glued to the TV, and Tina whispered, "Another bad day on Wall Street."

The Croc snapped, "Tina, get me a Scotch," then looked at me and pinched her nose. "And get that rancid waif out of here!"

When we got to the front door, Tina said, "Sammy, I really don't think she'll call the housing authority...not unless you make her really mad about something." She laughed. "And look at you! I mean, it's not like you're not trying."

"Well, what's going to happen on Friday if I don't find Marique?"

"Don't tell her I said this," she whispered, "but she'll pay it." She shook her head. "It'll about kill her, but she'll pay it."

"That's a lot of money for a dog!"

She looked over her shoulder at her mother in the den. "She's in there right now, trying to decide which stocks to sell."

"Tina!"

Tina rolled her eyes. "I'd better go get her that Scotch." The door *be-boop*ed as she opened it for me. "Don't sweat it so much. As long as she gets Marique back alive, everything'll be all right."

That did make me feel a little better. I didn't quite believe it, but I did feel better. And walking down their circular drive I realized that I was never going to make it home if I didn't get out of my jeans. The backs of my legs and my rear end were burning, and in the time it was going to take me to get home I'd be raw. I went over to the McKenzes', praying that Marissa was home.

She was. She took one look at me and said, "What *happened?*"

I stepped into the house and said, "Got caught digging through garbage, chased by a human bear, and hosed down with ammonia...you know, the usual."

She laughed. "Silly me. I thought you'd just been run over by a truck."

"I was hoping I could maybe take a shower?" I practically got on my knees. "Pleeeease?"

She laughed, "Yes, please! I'll get you some clean clothes." As I followed her down the hall, she said, "Don't let my mom see you. She'll call the exterminator."

"She's home again?"

"Miracle, huh? She's doing something in there with broccoli and pine nuts."

"Pine nuts?"

She rolled her eyes. "You got me."

She led me to the bathroom, and let me tell you, a shower never felt so good. I put on some of Marissa's clothes, and when I emerged she said, "I was going to wash your clothes, but Mom says they're hopeless. I threw them out, okay? You can have those."

I laughed. "Thank you."

"She wants to know if you want to stay for dinner."

"For broccoli and pine nuts?"

She practically got down on a knee. "Pleeeease?"

Well, I wouldn't play squirrel for just anyone, but for Marissa? I laughed and said, "Okay."

Grams wasn't too happy about me missing dinner for the second night in a row, but she tried to cover up and told me to have a good time. And I felt kind of bad, not telling her about Mrs. Graybill, but really, I didn't want to go through it right then. Not over the phone.

When I hung up, Mrs. McKenze says from over by the stove, "I've been thinking a lot about Lilia since you were

136

here the other day. Are you still having trouble with her?"

I nodded.

"Well, I had lunch with a friend, and her name came up."

"Oh?"

She shook some Parmesan cheese over the broccoli. "She wouldn't tell me much, but she did let it slip that Lilia's taken a second out on her house."

"A second? What's that?"

"A second mortgage. She's borrowing against the equity in her house."

I thought about this a minute. "She doesn't *own* that house?"

"Free and clear? Not anymore. I was under the impression that she paid cash for it originally, but if this is a *second*, then she probably doesn't have much equity left." She went back to sprinkling cheese. "I found it interesting."

I sat down on a stool at the breakfast bar and thought. About the Crocodile in her den watching her stocks. About her taking a second mortgage out on her house. About Tina cutting out coupons. And I wondered— would Mrs. Landvogt really pay fifty thousand dollars to get Marique back? And why, if Tina had had to cut out coupons in college, did she seem to think her mother would fork over that much money for a dog?

But the more I thought about it, the more I got the feeling that maybe Tina was right. It seemed that nothing mattered more to the Crocodile than her dog, so maybe she really would pay fifty thousand dollars to get Marique back.

If she could.

SIXTEEN

Grams was stunned. "She's dead? How can she be dead? She was here less than a week ago, cranky as ever." She kind of deflated into the couch. "I called there twice today, but both times they told me she was asleep. Oh, why didn't I just go over there?"

I said, "Don't be so hard on yourself, Grams, you couldn't have known...." Then I rested my head on her shoulder, and we just sat there for the longest time, not saying anything.

We went to bed early, but I don't think either of us got much sleep. And the next morning I was so tired that I almost asked Grams if I could stay home from school. Then I remembered Heather. I had one more day of following her around, and then it was up to Officer Borsch. If I could get ahold of him.

So I got up, got dressed, and walked out of the building like I lived there. I stopped by Maynard's Market to get a copy of *Dirt Bike* magazine for Dirt Boy and headed off to school.

When I got to homeroom, I slipped the magazine into Rudy's desk, then hurried over to my own. There was nothing on Heather's desk, and when the bell rang she slipped into her seat and said, "Finally getting smart, huh?"

I just gave her my evil little smile.

She shot over her shoulder, "Get a life, would you?"

After homeroom I didn't let her out of my sight. I followed her everywhere. I even followed her into the bathroom so that when she came out of the stall, there I was, staring at her in the mirror.

When I found her hiding with Tenille and Monet behind the locker room at lunchtime, I sat down right next to her on the asphalt and stared at her.

She spilled her fries trying to get away from me, crying, "What are you *doing*?"

One of her fries had fallen into my lap, so I popped it into my mouth and just sat there, chewing.

Tenille got up and said, "C'mon, Heather, let's go."

I made my little *tick-tock* sound and Heather said, "You're crazy, you know that? If you hurt me...If you lay even one finger on me ..."

They hauled her off while I *tick-tock*ed, a little louder.

By the end of school I was pretty sure that I couldn't ruffle her up much more than I already had, and I was starting to get worried that Officer Borsch wouldn't go along with my plan. What I had in mind was a long shot, and Officer Borsch isn't the long shot type. He likes citing code and writing tickets, which I guess is at least safer than what I do. I mean, getting doused with ammonia by a brownie-eating bear is probably something Officer Borsch has never experienced in the course of an investigation.

Anyhow, after school I was planning to get Elyssa and then go straight over to the police station. But I got sidetracked. By the Gypsy.

She was waiting by the gate, wrapped up in a khaki skirt

and a gauzy shirt, and was still missing the soles of her sandals. She called, "Sammy! Sammy, over here!"

I kind of circled around her. "You don't look like you've got good news...."

She pulled me aside, saying, "You've got to tell me the truth—for your own sake. Did you call the health department?"

Right away I knew she meant on Palmer's. "No way!"

She looked up like she was talking to God. "I knew it. I knew you wouldn't do that." She looked back at me and said, "*They* think you did. You or that Landvogt lady."

"Well, *I* didn't."

"I believe you, but Palmer's is shut down indefinitely, and Royce has got Paula believin' that you and Rich Witch were behind it."

"But why would she want to shut down Palmer's? It's not like she'd ever *go* there." A little picture of the Croc trying to shoot pool in her turban and claws ran through my brain, and it made me shudder.

The Gypsy said, "Look, I can't answer that. They don't know I heard them talking—I just thought I should warn you; you gotta steer clear of both of them, girl. They're acting real skittery."

"Like they're mad? Or like they're trying to hide something?"

She shook her head. "Maybe both. It's hard to say."

"Did they say anything about the dog?"

"Not squat." She pulled the brim of her hat down. "But I know they were squabbling about money. Something about him paying off a loan."

"To her?"

"I don't think so. Paula's been known to skate in the shade, so I think it's more like she's connected him with someone."

"Skate in the shade?"

"Not with the Mob, just loan sharks—that kind of scene. If Royce is tight for cash he might've bit the bait— who knows? It sure would explain why he's so jumpy, poking a gun in your face like that." She looked over her shoulder like she was afraid someone was following her. "Hey, I gotta boogie. You never saw me, right? I don't like feeling like a narc. I was just worried about you."

She started across the street, and I called, "Hey!"

She turned around. "Yeah?"

"Um...thanks."

She pointed a finger at me like a gun. "Eight ball, corner pocket. Sink it." Her hand jerked back like she'd fired, then she turned and hustled across the street.

I watched her go, wondering what she'd meant by that. Sink it. Finally I shook my head and started trotting out to Landview Elementary.

Elyssa didn't jump up when she saw me. She dragged her lunchbox down the steps and said, "I thought you weren't going to come."

I put out my hand and said, "Of course I came."

She let out a little sigh and put her hand in mine. "I thought you might still be crying."

I stopped and squatted down to look at her. "I'm sorry. I wish you hadn't seen me be so upset."

Her eyes looked so clear. So open. "Do you miss her?"

"Mrs. Graybill?"

"Uh-huh."

I started walking again and decided: there's no way I should talk depressing stuff around Elyssa. I looked at her and said, "Mrs. Graybill was the crabbiest old lady I ever knew."

"She *was*?" Her eyes were like two big buttons.

"And *nosy*. She was nosier than a...than an elephant!"

She giggled. "She was?"

"Uh-huh. Do you know what she used to do?"

"What?!"

So I went on and on about Mrs. Graybill, and to tell you the truth, it made *me* feel better, talking about her. And I was so busy talking that I completely forgot about seeing Officer Borsch until we were nearly past the mall.

"Oh hey, I forgot! I've got to go see Officer Borsch."

"Again?"

"He wasn't there yesterday, remember?"

She looked down and whispered, "I don't want to go."

"It'll be like yesterday. Just for a minute."

She looked up at me. "Promise?"

"Promise."

"All right," she said, but she was still pouting.

So we went to the police station and she waited outside, just like the day before. And behind the counter was the Dodo, carrying around that nest, just like the day before. The Dodo smiled and said, "You're back."

I nodded. "Is he here?"

"Floating around somewhere—let me go find him."

She went around a pillar and I could hear her, buzzing

him on an intercom. She came back and said, "He'll be here in a few. He's powdering his nose."

I looked through the window at Elyssa sitting on the bench and said, "Maybe I'll wait outside."

She looked at me looking at Elyssa and did a double take. "Say, isn't that Jim's little girl?"

"Jim?"

"What's her name? Eliza?"

"Elyssa."

"Yeah, that's it." She shook her head and sighed. "What a tragedy."

It took me a minute. "He's...dead?" I felt like a moron asking.

She shuddered. "Unfortunately. Bust gone bad over on the west side. It was a messy one." She took a deep breath, then let it out, saying, "What a great guy he was."

"How long ago was this?"

"Oh, it's been a year by now but it feels like yesterday. I've never seen so many people at a burial. It was like that whole new section of the cemetery was covered in black." She looked out the window again. "You can never tell when your marker's gonna come due."

Just then Officer Borsch walked through the door, but I wasn't thinking about cats anymore, I was thinking about Elyssa. I whispered to him, "I didn't know Elyssa's dad was a cop."

He nodded. "And a good one."

"Were you there when he got killed?"

He nodded again, then muttered, "And I've been back practically every night since."

I didn't have to ask. I know what bad dreams are like. "Is that why she runs away?"

"Elyssa? No. Well, I don't think so. She was pretty much sheltered from the whole thing. Didn't even attend the funeral."

"Why not?"

He shrugged. "She was so young...the department's psychologist didn't think it'd be a good idea."

"Oh."

"Anyway, I'm told you have some information about the cats?"

I let out a big breath and almost said, Forget it. I mean, all of a sudden the idea seemed really, really stupid.

"Well?"

I shook my head. "Promise you won't laugh, okay?"

He laughed and said, "No...," which for some reason tickled my funny bone. I laughed along with him and said, "All right, then just hear me out." I showed him the Polaroid pictures and said, "See this girl? Her name's Heather Acosta and she goes to my school. I'm about ninety-five percent sure she and her friends threw the cats."

"No proof?"

I shook my head. "And grilling her under your little hundred-watt bulb in there won't get you anywhere."

His lip tried to curl up under his nose. "Ninety-five percent isn't good enough."

"I know. Which is why I'm here. The other five percent is up to you."

So I told him about Hudson and "The Tell-Tale Heart," and since he didn't know the story, I had to tell

144

him about the guy hiding the body under the floorboards and all of that. And I'm right in the middle of the guy losing it in front of the policemen when Ol' Borsch-head practically breaks down and cries, "Samantha...! Do we really have to go through all this?"

"I'm sorry, but you have to know the story or this doesn't make any sense!"

"I get the picture already! Now can we get to the cats?"

So I told him about what I'd been doing at school and how Heather turned into a basket case whenever she saw me, and then I told him what I wanted him to do at the Christmas party the next day. He just closed his eyes and pinched the bridge of his nose. Finally he said, "It won't work. There is no way that's going to work."

"It's worth a try, don't you think?"

He shook his head. "No. It's ridiculous. It'll never work. How can you even *think* that's gonna work?"

Now, I knew it was kind of a crazy idea, but my feelings were still hurt. I mean there he was, being the Borsch-head I know and hate, treating me like a stupid little kid again. I headed for the door and said, "Fine. I don't see you coming up with a better idea, so you can just *giddy-up!*"

In the time it took me to cross the room and walk through the door I went from ninety-eight degrees to about a hundred and ten. And I started to tell Elyssa that she was right—Gil Borsch was a jerk and I hated his guts, but I couldn't.

She was gone.

SEVENTEEN

She was *gone* gone. I ran down Cook Street a ways looking like crazy for her and calling her name, then I turned around and started running in the other direction. I crossed over Cook Street and asked some people at the SMAT bus stop if they'd seen her, but they all looked at me like I was from Pluto. I went into the parking structure of the mall and called, "Elyssa!" but her name just bounced around inside until it faded away.

I thought about going back inside the police station and getting Officer Borsch, but I was still so mad at him that I couldn't. Besides, I thought I could still catch up with Elyssa if I tried. I headed up Cook Street, thinking that maybe she'd gotten tired of waiting and was on her way to the nursing home.

So I'm trying to convince myself that that's where she's got to be, but inside I'm panicking. Not like I've lost somebody's dog—much worse than that. Like somehow by making Elyssa wait in front of the police station I'd lost a friend. And somewhere in the stew of thoughts sloshing around in my brain I thought about what the Dodo and Officer Borsch had said about her dad, and all of a sudden it hit me where Elyssa must be. I hung a right and started running to Stowell Road.

Stowell is kind of a spooky street. It doesn't look that way if you're cruising along not thinking about things—it just looks like a regular street that could use a couple extra lanes to help with the traffic. But when you *do* think about it you get the creeps and start to avoid it.

See, on the far end of Stowell they have a medical building where all the obstetricians in town work. Next to that is a birthing center, and next to *that* is the hospital. The hospital takes up about two blocks and it's not painted black or anything. It's just a hospital. But what comes after the hospital is a nursing home, and on the other side of the nursing home is a mortuary. And then, across the next intersection, well, there's the cemetery. You could live your whole life on Stowell Road. Get born on one end, get buried on the other. Sure, you can take a little detour and go to school if you want, but pretty much it's all right there, in a row, on Stowell.

I'd never actually gone *into* the cemetery before. I'd looked at the backs of stone angels and statues poking up above the wall, but I'd never gone in to look at them face-to-face. So I wasn't sure where the entrance was, and I wound up walking clear down the block and around the corner.

When I did find a gate, I could tell it wasn't the main way in, but since it was open a bit, I kind of wedged my way through it.

I knew right away that I wasn't in the section the Dodo had been talking about. There was absolutely nothing new about it. The tombstones were big and heavy-looking—like they might sink right in if it started to rain. And the walkway was smooth and damp, covered with a thin layer of moss that slimed under my high-tops as I walked.

I turned and looked behind me, and there were my footsteps, following me. Then I noticed that the tombstones had black moss growing in the letters and across the crests. I read some of the stones, and when I got to one that read LYMAN URICH TOONEY, 1864–1906, the O's in *Tooney* seemed to stare at me like two eyes with heavy bags beneath them. And when I looked around, the O's and U's on all the tombstones seemed to pop out. Like a gallery of sleepless eyes, watching me.

I slip-slided my way out of there as fast as I could. And I was trying to decide which way to go at a Y in the path when I heard, "You seem a tad confused, missy. Lookin' for anyone in particular?"

Now it wasn't dark yet, but it *felt* dark. There were old crusty trees arching over the pathway, making it kind of shadowy. And even though the path was a little drier than it had been back by the Tooney tomb, I still didn't have much traction, and I couldn't exactly run. And hearing this voice come out of nowhere, well, all I wanted to *do* was run. I mean, it sounded like someone coming up from underground to lend me a hand.

The voice came again. "Not really supposed to use that gate no more, missy. Waiting on a hinge to seal it up."

Then I spotted him, leaning against a tree with a hoe in one hand. He looked greasy and dusty. Like a raven that had been bathing in soot. He pushed himself off the tree trunk and hobbled over to the foot of a grave, saying, "If

you're after some relation I can prob'ly help ya." He
started hoeing away at a tall weed. "But if you're just takin'
a shortcut home you best go out the way you came."

"I'm not taking a shortcut, sir, I...I'm here to find—"

He perked right up. "What's the name?"

"Uh, Sammy Keyes."

His lips pushed way out, and then he looked up, like he
was kissing the sky. "Must be in the new section. You got
a plot number by chance?"

"A what?"

He hobbled onto the grave and started whacking away
at another weed. "A plot number. Don't matter, we can
go look it up. I just don't recall no Samuel Keyes."

"Oh no, sir! *I'm* Sammy Keyes."

He leaned on the hoe, holding it with both hands.
"You're looking for your own plot?"

"No sir, I..." I closed my eyes and took a deep breath.
"I'm looking for the gravesite of Jim Keltner. He was a
policeman who died about a year ago."

He smiled and said, "Now, *that* I can help you with."
He leaned the hoe against a cement angel. "You a relation
of Lyssie's, by chance?"

I followed him down the path. "Elyssa? No. I'm...I'm
her friend."

"Good," he said as he studied me. "Very good."

So I followed him through the cemetery. And it was
strange—the place went from being a moss garden with
trees and sagging tombstones to a place in the sun with
straight rows, no trees, and flat grave markers. It was like
wandering through an antique store full of old oak rocking

chairs and armoires and then turning in to a room with plastic furniture. It just didn't seem to fit.

Ol' Dusty must have known what I was thinking because he says, "It'll look a whole lot better once those saplings take. That there's an olive, those along there are plum— we're gonna alternate 'em all the way out to the end of the district. Even before we open the next section up. Give it ten years—it'll be nice."

So while he's chattering away about the cemetery's ten-year expansion plan, my heart's letting out a sigh of relief because clear across the lawn I can see a little girl by a grave and there's no doubt about it—it's my runaway elf.

I say, "Thanks," and start walking a little faster, but Dusty keeps hobbling right alongside me. When we get to the gravesite, Elyssa's sitting cross-legged, picking blades of grass out, one by one, and placing them on the marker. She looks up and says, "Oh, hi, Mike. Hi, Sammy," like we were just passing by.

"You doin' okay today, Lyssie?"

She shrugs and snaps off another blade of grass.

"Well, you got company so I best be goin'."

Elyssa waves and we both watch him hobble away. Then she goes back to yanking grass and says, "Mike's nice."

I sat down next to her and watched her for a minute. She didn't really look upset—she was just concentrating on those blades of grass. Finally I said, "So this is where you go."

She shrugged. "Usually."

A motor started up somewhere in the distance. "Even after dark?"

"Sometimes. Usually I leave when it gets dark." She looked over her shoulder and started picking up the blades of grass.

A riding mower was purring around by the main gate. After a minute it came our way, cutting grass along the fence. We both watched it awhile, and finally I said, "They mow right over the graves?"

She nodded. "Mike says that's why you can't have statues anymore." The mower was almost straight ahead of us now. "You can't plant flowers, either."

"Because they have to mow?"

She stared at the gardener. "I don't like it."

No, I was thinking, neither do I.

So we sat there, watching the gardener, and before too long the entire new section was mowed. All except for a big circle around Jim Keltner's grave.

When the gardener was gone, I looked at her and said, "So why don't you want your mom to know you come here?"

She started putting her blades of grass back on the grave. "She doesn't know I know."

"That he...that he's here?"

She nodded, then looked at me. "She wants me to think he's in heaven."

"Well, I'm sure he is...."

Her eyes shot straight for mine. "But yesterday you said you didn't know where Mrs. Graybill was! You said no one knows!"

Uh-oh, I was thinking, Uh-*oh*. "Well, I...I mean..."

"And when I asked Hudson where heaven was, he

showed me the moon and all the stars and told me it was up there. But he called them the heavens and said they go on and on forever!"

"Hudson was probably trying to explain about the universe. He—"

"And Miss Ugalde told me that the angels came for him. Shane says there's no such thing as angels, but Miss Ugalde promised! She told me how beautiful they are and how nice they are and how Daddy's safe with them. So I watch and I watch and I wait and I wait, but I've never seen one. Not one." She looked straight at me. "Have *you* ever seen one?"

I looked into her big brown eyes and I wished with all my heart that I could say yes, but there went my head, shaking back and forth. I tried to make the boulder in my throat disappear by forcing out a laugh. "'Course, I've never really *looked*, either."

The boulder didn't budge.

She didn't think it was too funny, either. "So where is he?" She pointed to the sky, falling into darkness. "Is he up there? Is he with the angels?" She looked back at the gravesite and whispered, "Or is he in there?"

I hadn't realized until then that across the marker she had pieced together the word *Daddy* with her blades of grass. She looked at me and whispered, "Where *is* he?"

I didn't know what to say. Nothing much was going to make it past that boulder anyway. And I don't know why, because I'd never really thought of it this way before, but I reached over, touched her chest, and said, "He's right in there."

She blinked at me a minute, so I nodded and said it again, "Right in there, Elyssa. Always."

They started one by one, scared little tears popping from her eyes. Then all of a sudden she let them go. All of them. She buried her face in my sweatshirt, and while she was busy soaking it, I dripped all over the top of her head. And somewhere in the middle of all that crying I looked up at the sky, and there was the moon, just starting to shine through the dusk. And it felt like the distant light of a projector, beaming a ray of hope into my heart.

Maybe Elyssa wouldn't need to be the Runaway Elf anymore.

EIGHTEEN

It was Elyssa's bedtime when I finally left the Keltners'. Mrs. Keltner gave me a hug on the porch and said, "How can I ever thank you?"

I shrugged and nudged a pebble around with my hightop. I mean, she'd already thanked me about a billion times, and I didn't feel like I'd really *done* anything. Then I had a great idea. I peeked around her to make sure Elyssa hadn't sneaked out of bed. "Get her a sheepdog."

"A...*sheepdog?*"

I smiled real big and nodded.

"As if there isn't enough chaos in my life." Her head was shaking and her face was hidden behind a hand. Finally she peeked at me through her fingers and said, "A sheepdog..."

"Maybe for Christmas?"

She let out a sigh. "What am I going to do with a sheepdog?"

I chased that pebble around some more and said, "It would make her really happy." I looked up. "She'd also probably race right home after school."

Mrs. Keltner was looking off into the distance, nodding. "A sheepdog."

"If you got it as a puppy she could train it and..."

She wasn't listening. "A sheepdog!" I thought she was going to tousle my hair. "Thank you! This is going to be the best possible Christmas." She turned around like I'd already left, smiling to herself, murmuring, "A sheepdog!"

The Keltners' porch light clicked off and I could see their Christmas tree shining through the curtains of the living room. I stood there a minute, kind of grinning, and then I headed down the walkway.

There was too much jumbling around inside me to go home before I sorted it out a bit, and since I'd already called Grams, I wasn't worried about her being worried about me. I was more worried that Hudson wouldn't be there to talk to.

But he was there, all right. In the dark. Boots up, cocoa steaming. I couldn't see his face, but I knew he was smiling. "Well, look who's here!"

"Hi, Hudson."

"Got time for some cocoa?"

I sat down next to him. "You bet."

He brought out a cup and poured some from his thermos, saying, "Rita tells me your mother's coming into town."

I'd completely forgotten. "Oh, yeah."

He eyed me. "Had a hunch you wouldn't be doing a jig."

I just sighed.

He looked out at the moon. "It's one of those choppy passages you have to negotiate, whether you want to or not. You can decide to go around the rocks or face them head-on. Either way, you have to get from here to there."

Normally I would've given him an argument—or at least told him I didn't want to get from here to there—but for some reason I was just quiet. Then he asked, "What about Mrs. Graybill? How is she?"

The words kind of stuck in my throat. "She's dead."

He stopped midslurp. "Good Lord! Seriously?"

I nodded, and then very quietly I told him all about it. How she'd called my name all day, how she'd begged me to forgive her, and how all of a sudden, there she was, gone forever.

He was quiet for a long time and then his head started moving back and forth a little. Pretty soon it had gained some serious momentum. "Unbelievable. Just unbelievable."

I whispered, "I never thought I'd cry over Mrs. Graybill."

"I take it you did?"

I nodded and told him how it felt like someone had ripped my heart out when I'd figured out she was dead. Then I told him about what I'd said when Elyssa had found me crying, and before you know it I'm going on and on about mossy tombstones and riding mowers. And when I'm finally done telling him what happened at the gravesite, he lets out a low whistle and says, "That poor child!" He sat up a bit. "I feel awful for contributing to her confusion. I barely even remember her asking about heaven."

I watched him gazing out at the stars and whispered, "Do you really believe in heaven?"

Now you have to understand—Hudson goes to St. Mary's Church every Sunday, and even though we've

156

spent all kinds of time talking about Father Mayhew and his carrot-eating dog and why the sisters who work the soup kitchen are so crabby, he's never really talked to me about God or heaven or believing. So the minute I heard myself ask the question I was sorry because I didn't want Hudson to talk about God and heaven and believing. I get plenty of that from Father Mayhew.

I almost said, Whoops! I take that back—never mind! but before I could, Hudson nods and says, "I believe what you're asking is, Is the end of life a period? Or merely a comma?" He turns to me. "I don't have the answer, but I do know that what you believe should give you comfort. What you told little Elyssa today is the heart of the truth, and that's what matters. About the rest, just keep your mind open. You'll find that conclusions tend to evolve if you let them."

My brain was busy digesting this when he says, "Well, would you look at that." He points to the house across the street. "The Cranstons broke down and bought a tree."

I could see lights coming to life through the living room window. "Don't they usually get a tree?"

Hudson tugged on an eyebrow and gave me a sly little smile. "Didn't you know? Only heathens get trees." He kicked his boots up on the railing and chuckled. "I guess that little grandson coming to visit's finally turned them around."

The lights suddenly went out, then came back on again. Not like twinkling lights—more like lights with a loose connection. Hudson chuckled again and said, "Now they're sending out Morse code to Santa!"

We laughed about that for a while, and then I forced myself to get up. "I better get going."

On the way down the steps my heart felt really heavy because I knew—it was too late. My last night to find Marique was gone, and unless I got really lucky and the Crocodile *didn't* call the housing authorities, I wouldn't have to worry about giving the GasAway Lady the couch—there wouldn't *be* a couch.

I looked back at Hudson and asked, "How would you feel about lending me your couch for a few weeks?" thinking that if the Crocodile *did* call, at least Grams stood a chance of not getting kicked out if no one could find me.

Hudson nodded and said, "You're always welcome," but he eyed me over his cocoa mug and added, "Keep in mind, though, that if you're determined to fight your way upstream, at least go between the rocks. Your vessel will last longer."

I blinked at him and then realized that he was thinking *I* was thinking about my mother. I said, "Okay, I will," and then, as I'm going down the steps, I have a terrible thought. "Do I have to buy her a present?"

He chuckles and shakes his head. "A present that's not from the heart is no present at all, Sammy."

"So does that mean I *don't*?"

His head was still shaking. "That's up to you."

So I head home, worrying about the GasAway Lady and Christmas, thinking how *Grams* is the person I want to get something special for, but what she'll probably wind up getting from me is an eviction notice. Then I start thinking how hiding out at Hudson's might actually be

158

kind of fun because I could spend more time on his porch watching the world go by. Well, *that* gets me thinking about watching the Cranstons sending out Morse code to Santa, and then all of a sudden I get a little lightheaded, and pretty soon I feel like I'm walking on the moon.

I sit right down on the curb, and while I'm feeling like a puff of cloud that's strayed from the storm, my brain is throwing thunderbolts back and forth inside my skull. It finally rumbles to a stop, and what I'm left with is something that *almost* makes sense.

I got up and ran. As hard as I could, as fast as I could. All the way to the Pup Parlor. And I rang that bell until I thought it was going to buzz itself right off the wall.

Holly comes charging down the stairs, and when she sees it's me she throws open the door and says, "What's wrong?"

"Is Vera here?"

"She's just getting ready for bed."

I went charging up the stairs calling over my shoulder, "Does she have any pictures of the parade?"

"What?"

I practically knocked Vera over at the top of the stairs. "Vera! Did you get your parade pictures developed?"

"Uh, yes. I did." She shuffled over to the kitchen counter. "They're right here."

I was shaking as I took them out of the package. "Did you shoot them from the mall side or from across the street?"

"From across the street."

I was already flipping through the pictures. "Where?"

159

"A little ways up from Cook."

My heart was pounding. "Good."

Holly whispered, "What's going on?"

"I think I know who has Marique."

Holly and Vera said, "You do?"

I flipped through the pictures fast once, then more slowly. Vera pointed over my shoulder. "You like that one? They're all flying off."

I backed up one. "Are these in order?"

"Should be."

I backed up another and studied it. "Do you have a magnifying glass?"

"I have a loupe."

I looked up at her. "What's a loupe?"

Vera shrugged and said, "It's like a magnifying glass for photos. You want it?"

"Yes!"

She came back a minute later and handed me something that looked like a squatty little hourglass with a band around the top. She said, "Here, let me turn on the light."

I held the loupe up to my eye, then bent over the photograph. Five seconds later, I was positive who had Marique.

NINETEEN

It took a bit of talking to convince Vera to let Holly come with me, but in the end she said okay *if* Marissa went with us and *if* we promised not to go inside and *if* we called if we weren't going to be home by ten o'clock. We just said yeah, yeah, yeah and went charging out of there.

The whole way over to Marissa's we talked about what we were going to do and how we were going to do it, and by the time we were pounding on Marissa's door I knew there was no way around it—I was going to have to break one of my promises.

Marissa did a bit of the McKenze dance when we told her what was going on, but when I started talking about how I had to get inside, Holly said, "Wait a minute! We promised we wouldn't do that."

"And *you* don't have to. But there's something I have to get, otherwise this'll never be over." I finished explaining what I wanted to do, then borrowed a little penlight from Marissa, and off we went to the Landvogt mansion. Marissa and Holly went up to the front door while I climbed over the back fence.

Now, maybe I could've done the whole thing myself, but I didn't want to be snooping around the Crocodile's back door while she or Tina were in the kitchen, looking for a late-night snack. Besides, I wasn't really sure I could get inside, and I sure didn't want to get caught halfway.

I tiptoed up the back steps and held my breath as I pushed Marique's doggy door open a few inches. No alarm. I put my ear up to the crack and waited for the doorbell to ring, and when it did, I got ready. I pushed the doggy door open as far as I could, and then when I heard the opening alarm *be-boop*, I wrestled my head and one arm in and reached up as high as I could. The deadbolt was about four inches away.

I squirmed in a little farther and tried again. It was still at least an inch out of reach. I crammed myself in until it felt like the door was going to cut through my ribs. This time I managed to snap the deadbolt back.

Getting myself back out of the doggy door felt like pulling a sword from my side, but I just tried to ignore how much it hurt and got ready. I put one hand on the doorknob, my ear to the doggy door, and waited.

I knew that when she closed the front door I'd have only a split second, and even then she might notice. So the instant the closing chime began, I pushed open the back door and my *be-boop* kind of harmonized over her *bo-beep*.

Now I couldn't shut the door. The closing chime would sound again and I'd give myself away. So I turned on my penlight and tiptoed into the pantry, and there was the alarm panel on the wall, blinking away. I flipped the switch over to Deactivate, then tiptoed out and closed the back door. No alarm.

So there I am, sneaking through the Crocodile's kitchen, carrying my penlight like a match in a refinery, and I'm just passing the island when I hear the purr of a crocodile on wheels.

I pop the penlight off and duck. Then suddenly fluorescent lights flood the kitchen, and I can hear her, wheeling across the tile floor. My heart's trying to whack a great big hole through my chest, but my feet won't budge. It's like they're cemented to the floor.

She rolls right up to the far counter, pulls a glass out of the dishwasher, and then stands up. Just like that, she's up and hobbling around. Now let me tell you, it's a scary sight seeing a crocodile get up on its back legs and walk. It's like seeing a boa constrictor fly. One minute you're thinking that if you keep your distance you'll be all right, and the next minute you're realizing that you need to switch continents to survive.

From where I'm crouched she looks about ten feet tall, and she's *fast*. She hobbles over to a cupboard and brings down some pretzels, then she kind of sashays over to the refrigerator for a bottle of seltzer water. And while she's getting down a bowl for the pretzels I notice her big black book, just sitting there in her wheelchair.

Now, I'm not suicidal. Really I'm not. It's just that sometimes part of my brain wants me to act that way, and it takes everything I've got to stop it. And I'm there, in the middle of talking myself down from charging that wheelchair, when the phone rings. I jump back a bit, and as she hobbles over to the phone, I keep one eye on her and the other glued to that big black book sitting all by itself in her chair.

The Croc picks up the phone and says, "Yes?" then

turns her back and waits for a second. Finally she says, "Well, *why* was I crossed off the list?"

It was too late to turn back. I was already inching my way into open ground.

"That makes no sense. I've been invited to the Christmas Ball every year for the past ten years! I was even on the *committee* last year. You need to find out why."

I was trying to move slowly so she wouldn't notice me out of the corner of her eye, but with my heart slamming around inside me like a Bumble Ball, it wasn't easy. Then, when she said, "Wait a minute, *Nora* said that? Nora Hallenback?" I froze. And if I hadn't been so petrified I might have smiled. The Landvogt Empire was starting to crumble. All I needed was that book!

I crawled the rest of the way to the wheelchair, and suddenly there it was, in my hand—my ticket off Crocodile Isle, my guidebook to independence, my antiblackmail blackmail.

The Croc twisted the top off her seltzer water, and I could tell that any second she'd twist her *head* and I'd be caught. So instead of going back the way I'd come, I ducked beside another counter and rolled into a hallway.

I heard the phone slam down, so I scrambled a little farther down the hallway and held my breath. A minute later the fluorescent lights went off, and all of a sudden there I was, alone in the dark.

When my eyes got adjusted a bit, I started noticing things. Like the carpet—it wasn't thick and bouncy. It was low and sturdy. Almost industrial. And the doors— they weren't paneled wood like the rest of the house.

They were flat and painted. But what really gave away that I was in the low-rent part of the house was that there was no chandelier. Just a regular ceiling light.

I was ready to take that blackmailer's bible and hightail it out of there, but Tina had said she lived downstairs in the servants' quarters, and I was thinking that one of these rooms might be Tina's.

I started at the back end of the hallway and worked my way up. Each room was cold and either empty or full of junk. Persian rugs, antique chairs, Tiffany lamps—you know, junk.

Then I opened the room closest to the kitchen and right away I knew it was Tina's. For one thing, I didn't feel a blast of cold air when I opened the door. For another, I recognized her red jacket sitting right there on the bed.

I left the door open a crack and started snooping around with my penlight. The bed wasn't much bigger than a cot, and wedged between it and the wall was a worn recliner. There was a desk with two drawers, but there was nothing in them. Just pens and pencils and some old magazines. And as I looked around at the bare walls, it hit me that the room didn't feel like someone actually *lived* in it. It felt more like a prison cell.

I rummaged through the dresser and there were clothes all right, but not what you'd expect in a rich girl's wardrobe. Mostly jeans and sweatshirts and socks. I looked under the bed pillow and then the mattress, but there was nothing stashed under them. And the more I looked around, the more panicky I got. I mean, Vera's picture might have convinced *me*, but it probably wasn't enough to convince anybody else. Especially if they didn't want to believe.

So I started looking again, and that's when I thought to check out the jacket. I picked it off the bed and stuck my hand in a pocket. It was empty, but I could feel something heavy in an inside pocket. I groped around, and what I found was a little tape recorder. I put it down on the bed and started going through the jacket again. I could hear a piece of paper crumpling around in the lining somewhere, but I couldn't seem to figure out which pocket it was in. Then, just as I found it, I heard, "I forgot my jacket, that's why!"

I yanked the paper out and threw the jacket on the bed. Then I scooped up the black book and the recorder and dived into the closet. A second later, Tina comes in, grabs her jacket, and leaves.

I wait until it's quiet, then I push the penlight on and unfold the paper. And what I'm sitting there holding is a receipt. A kennel receipt. I stuff it in my sweatshirt pocket along with Vera's picture, and then check out the buttons on the recorder. I press Rewind, then Play, and after a few seconds of static, "Maaaariiique! Maaaariiique!" fills the closet. I snap down the Stop button as fast as I can, then put the recorder with the receipt and picture.

All that's left is the Croc's bible, and when I open it up, what I see is amazing. It's like FBI notes. There's the name of the person, their Social Security number, address, phone number, where they bank, their maiden name, their mother's maiden name—information like that, and then pages of notes about every person. Gossipy things. Cruel things.

I should have closed the book and gotten out of there, but it was like reading the devil's bible. There was dirt on Mayor Hibbs, there was dirt on the superintendent of schools and the chief of police. You name someone important in Santa Martina, and she had *something* on them. And the more I read, the more I knew, I now had something on *her*.

I closed the book and was just getting up when Tina's bedroom door flew open and the light flicked on.

I had closed the closet door the best I could, but it was still open a few inches, and I didn't dare move it any more. Tina came charging in and searched the floor and around the bedspread. I held my breath and inched my way backward, trying to find something to hide beneath, but her closet was so empty that it was like trying to hide behind a miniskirt. And I'm just getting ready to pull down some clothes to cover myself, when I hear the Croc roll in.

"Mother! What are you doing back here?"

The Croc studies her and says, "I thought you said you were leaving."

"I left! I just came back because I'm...I'm missing something."

"Missing something?"

"My...my wallet. I was sure I left it in my jacket."

I could see those crocodile eyes squeeze together. "Don't lie to me, child."

Tina looks down and then checks under her bed again. "I'm not lying."

"I've always been able to read you like a book, Christina. You're lying."

"I never lie to you, Mother! I lie *for* you plenty, but not *to* you."

"Well, if you left and came back, why didn't I hear the annunciator?"

Tina just stands there, blinking. Then she whispers, "That's funny. Neither did I."

She goes charging out, and in the time it takes the Croc to turn around, Tina's back. "It's been turned off!"

"By?"

"Don't accuse me! Why would I turn off the alarm?"

"Well, it certainly didn't switch off by itself."

Tina checks the pockets of her jacket again. "Did you let anyone in while I was gone?"

"That girl from across the street came over with some sob story about giving Samantha more time. She was pretty persistent and she took up a bit of time, but I didn't let her in the house."

Tina stops patting her pockets. "Sammy's friend?" She sits down on the bed and the color disappears from her face. She whispers, "Sammy knows about the alarm."

"How the devil would she know about the alarm?"

"I asked her to get a lemon for me...." She looks up at her mother and chokes out, "She's in this house. She's somewhere in this house."

"Oh, that's nonsense! How could she get in past me?"

"I don't know, but I think we should get you up to your room."

"*What*? I'm not afraid of a twelve-year-old girl! If she's

168

managed to break into the house, so what? Tina, why are you so nervous?"

"Trust me, mother. Let's get you up to your room."

Well, let me tell you, my heart was slamming its way all over that closet. My chance for sneaking out of the Landvogt mansion had come and gone. I was trapped. Like a cuckoo in a clock. And with the big hand pointing straight up, there was only one thing to do.

Cuckoo.

TWENTY

I crammed the bible in the back waistband of my jeans, covered it with my sweatshirt, then opened the closet door and came out with both hands in the air.

Tina nearly fainted, but the Croc didn't even flinch. "What is the meaning of this? How dare you break into my house!"

"You wanted me to find Marique. I've found Marique."

"*What?* Well, where is she?"

I handed over the kennel receipt. "I think you'll find her at the Wag and Whisker in Santa Luisa."

She studied it, then handed it back. "This is a receipt for a dog named Bubbles!"

"My bet is that Bubbles is one bald little Pomeranian." I looked over at Tina. "Isn't it, Tina?"

Tina snatched the receipt and said, "You are really grasping. Bubbles is Buddy's grandmother's dog. She's visiting Buddy's sister for Christmas and she asked us to check Bubbles into the Wag and Whisker for her."

The Croc blinked. "Wait a minute. That's your receipt?"

"It sure is, and I don't know what she thinks she's doing saying that—"

I pressed the Play button, and "Maaaariiique! Maaaariiique!" filled the room.

"That's *my* voice," the Croc whispered.

"Exactly. Tina played it over Buddy's megaphone at the

parade. Marique heard it and that's why she went charging off the float."

Tina rolled her eyes. "Oh, you've got to be kidding! How farfetched can you get?"

I looked at her and said, "It never made sense to me because you were home when the ransom note came and you were home when the fur got delivered."

"That's right! Mother, she's just proved how ridiculous this whole theory is!"

I shook my head. "But then I remembered how both times you played with the lights on the Christmas tree. That was your signal to Buddy to make the delivery."

Mrs. Landvogt was turning a very odd shade of green. Even for a crocodile. "You and Buddy did this?"

"Mom, don't listen to her! There's no way I—"

"And then I remembered how the first time I came over you looked straight at Marissa and asked if she was Sammy."

"So *what*?"

"So if you'd been at the parade concentrating on anything besides getting your mitts on Marique, you'd have known *I* was Sammy, not Marissa."

"Oh, come on! Like I'm supposed to remember every twelve-year-old girl I run into. Besides, I *taped* the parade. That's proof right there that I didn't do it!"

I looked straight at Tina. "If you don't mind, I'm thirteen." I handed Mrs. Landvogt Vera's picture and said, "Here, take a magnifying glass to that and you'll see Buddy holding a video camera, not Tina."

She barely looked at it. "I don't need a magnifying glass. I recognize his jacket from here." Her voice sounded scratchy, almost tired. She glared at Tina and hissed, "How could you *do* this to me? You're my *daughter!*"

Tina knew there was no use denying it anymore. Instead, she went off like a rocket. "Your *daughter?* I'm not your daughter, I'm your slave! The only reason you want me around is so I can *do* things for you. You don't want to talk to me, you don't want to do things with me. You don't care how I feel or what I think or how you hurt me!"

"How I hurt *you?* What is this you've been doing to *me?* You've been blackmailing your own mother!"

Tina snickered, then said, "Like mother, like daughter. I learned from the master. You got a problem? Call immigration. Or the health department." Her eyes got really big. "Or better yet, the wife! I can't stand being in this town anymore. Everyone knows I'm just your little agent. People are *afraid* of me! Why? Because I'm Lilia Landvogt's daughter."

"A little fear is good for people. That's no reason to turn on the person who has housed you and supported you and loved you!"

"Loved me?" Tina choked out a laugh. "*Loved* me? Is that some kind of a joke? You don't love me. Ever since Yelsa got out you've hated me!"

The Crocodile blinked at her. "I haven't *hated* you..."

"Well, you've never forgiven me!"

The Croc shrugged and let out a little sigh. "Well, it *was* unforgivable. You should've been more responsible."

"I was *ten years old!*"

"Still."

Tina slid down the wall onto the floor. She wrapped her arms around her legs, buried her face in her knees, and burst into tears. And while she's rocking back and forth, sobbing, the Croc gives her a disgusted look and says to me, "Well, I guess you're off the hook."

I felt like kicking her leg. And standing there listening to her daughter's heart break while she sat there shaking her head made me want to yell at her about Mrs. Graybill and where a lack of forgiveness had gotten *her*.

But then I realized I wasn't dealing with Mrs. Graybill. I was dealing with a crocodile. A cold-blooded reptile with her very own cross-referenced blackmailer's bible.

I followed as she rolled over to the front door and opened it without a word. I stepped out, then turned and faced her from the porch. "I don't expect thanks, Mrs. Landvogt. I just expect to be left alone. And in case you ever get the idea that maybe you'd like to try blackmailing me again, well, don't."

She gave me a condescending little smile. "Oh, what's this now? A threat? Really, Samantha, what could you possibly do to me?"

I gave her a condescending little smile right back. "Let's just say that if my grandmother or I should ever run into difficulties with any sort of authorities, or if anything should mysteriously *happen* to either of us, *this* will become a very public document." I held up the black book and said, "You won't live to tell your side of it."

I think she swallowed her tongue. She choked and sputtered and her mouth went up and down like a seesaw. Finally she got right out of her wheelchair and started after me, but I was already gone. I was feeling so light and moving so fast that nothing, not even a posse of crocodiles, could've caught me.

TWENTY-ONE

I started reading the book that night. Among other things, I found out that the Gypsy was right about Mr. Petersen—he was in with loan sharks way over his head, and it turns out that Paula Nook's ex was one of them.

It was fascinating reading, but the deeper I got into it, the more I knew that there was only one thing I could do with the book. I had to burn it. It felt radioactive—like the longer I was near it, the more it would rot me from the inside out.

Hudson didn't even ask. He just opened the door at seven in the morning and lit me a fire. And when the book was done smoking its way up the chimney, he pointed to the three pages I had left in my hand and said, "I sense that's an insurance policy."

"Not for me. These two are for Mrs. Hallenback, and this one's for Officer Borsch."

Hudson raised an eyebrow. "Your pal on the force?"

I snorted, "Some pal," and was in the middle of telling him how Ol' Borsch-head wasn't even willing to try to help me trap Heather when all of a sudden I remembered I'd never gotten Rudy a present for the exchange party. "Oh no!"

"What's the matter, Sammy?"

"What am I going to do?"

"About Officer Borsch?"

"No!" I looked at him and asked, "You got anything that a guy who likes dirt might want for Christmas?"

Hudson gave me a worried look. "Dirt?"

"I'm Rudy Folksmeir's KK, and we're having an exchange party at the end of the day. I completely forgot to get him something."

"But dirt?"

I laughed and said, "He's way into dirt bikes."

"Ah...dirt bikes." He rubbed his chin a minute. "Why don't we check in the garage."

Hudson's garage is like a little operating room for his car, Jester. Jester's a 1960 sienna rose Cadillac that you'd better never describe as lavender. Jester doesn't drip oil or water or any other bodily fluids, and there's not a scratch on it.

Hudson flipped on the operating lights. "How about an oil can?"

"An *oil* can?"

"Any biker worth his dirt is going to appreciate one of these."

I was expecting a container of oil. Like what goes in an engine. What Hudson got down from a shelf, though, was a shiny copper can that looked like a cross between an inkwell and a candle holder. He handed it to me and said, "Most folks don't use them anymore, but I haven't found anything better for lubing joints and getting into tight places. Trust me, your friend Rudy will like it."

I laughed. "If you say so."

He winked at me. "I say so."

So we gave it a real festive wrap in a paper sack, and as I was stuffing it in my backpack he noticed my present for Heather, wrapped in shiny red paper. His eyebrows popped up a little. "For someone a little less dirt-conscious...?"

I laughed, then showed him how I'd wrapped the lid separate from the box and how Grams' old kitchen timer was sitting inside. He rubbed his chin a bit, so I gave the timer a twist, then put the box together. "It's for Heather."

He threw his head back and laughed. "Her tell-tale heart!"

I ran down his steps calling, "Wish me luck. I think I'm going to need it!"

The last day of school before Christmas vacation is probably the best day of the whole school year. You don't do anything academic—most teachers are smarter than that. Everyone's in a good mood because vacation's coming, Christmas is coming, and sugar is everywhere.

And at William Rose Junior High, they don't even make you go back to class after the gift exchange. You just hang out in the cafeteria for a while and then you get to go home.

Anyhow, by the time the gift exchange rolled around, Marissa, Holly, Dot, and I were so hyped up on candy canes and chocolate that we were actually excited about making idiots of ourselves in front of the whole school. And while the rest of the kids piled into the cafeteria to watch our vice principal, Mr. Caan, play the role of Santa, we snuck into the bathroom to get ready.

Holly and I checked the stalls to make sure there were no smokers standing on toilets waiting to flick their Bics, while Dot pulled out a tube of white face paint and Marissa emptied a sack of robes. She held one up and said, "Is this what you had in mind, Sammy?"

I couldn't believe it. "Those are perfect!"

She giggled. "I know!"

Holly put one on and flipped up the hood. "Where in the world did you find these?"

"My cousin Brandon. I guess at the high school they do this thing every year during Red Ribbon Week where the Students Against Drunk Driving dress up as Death. It's supposed to demonstrate how often people get killed by drunk drivers."

I put mine on and said, "These are *way* better than I expected."

Marissa grinned. "You wanted black, you got black."

Dot smeared our faces with white paint and then put heavy black circles under our eyes. Then she decided she wanted to paint our hands white and put some black around our fingernails. When we finally looked at each other in the mirror we jumped back a little. We looked scary!

I turned Grams' timer on and stuck it in the red box while Holly and Marissa got their empty presents ready. When we were done, Dot lined us up and said, "You guys are the scariest Three Kings I've ever seen!"

I laughed and said, "Remember, we have to take ourselves seriously or this will never work. We sure look like Death. Now all we have to do is act like Death and *think* like Death."

So we all practiced looking real serious and, you know, like Death. And after a few minutes of practicing, I said,

"Okay, Dot, you better wait by the front doors on the off chance Officer Borsch decides to show up."

She nodded and said, "If he comes, I'll get him to the cafeteria," then looked at her watch. "If you told him twelve-thirty we better hurry. It's twelve-thirty now."

The teachers in the cafeteria were so busy laughing at Santa Caan be-bopping to "Jingle Bell Rock" that they didn't even notice us walking by.

Heather didn't notice us either. We circled around her so that we could maneuver her toward the door, and it wasn't until we were about ten feet from her that Monet grabbed her arm and said, "Look!"

We didn't say a word, we just came at her, three across, with me out front a little. All of a sudden, "Jingle Bells" quit rocking and the cafeteria went quiet. I held my little red box out to Heather, and it seemed really loud, ticking away.

She took a few steps back and tried to laugh. "You guys are crazy…!" But we kept coming at her, slowly, with empty eyes.

Panic skated across her face, and I figured it was now or never. I held the box a little higher and said in a real monotone voice, "Heather Acosta, your time has come."

Heather put her hands up and said, "You guys have taken this way too seriously! It was just a prank, okay? Get over it!"

We kept coming.

"Hey, Sammy, back off! What are you doing? I'm sorry, okay?"

I kept coming at her.

She blinked a bunch, then looked over her shoulder for a place to run.

That's when she saw Officer Borsch. That's when *I* saw Officer Borsch. And for a minute I almost forgot I was playing Death and smiled. Heather took one last look at me, then charged over to him screaming, "Stop them! They're trying to kill me! They've got...they've got a bomb!"

Officer Borsch just stood there, rock-steady, not saying a word.

"Stop her! Oh my God, why don't you stop her!"

I kept coming.

He looked down at her and said, "Heather Acosta, your time has come."

She looked at him in disbelief and then got down on her knees and hugged his leg. "I didn't mean any harm! I said I was sorry! What more do you want?" She started crying. "You can't let them kill me over a few stupid cats!"

I took off my hood and smiled at Officer Borsch. "She's all yours."

Heather looked at him and then at me, and you could see it sinking in. I took the lid off my box and said, "I'd give you this as a gift, but really, I'm not your KK. I've heard Cindy Ruiz is. Besides, I've got to get this timer back to my grandmother. She's got pies to bake."

By now Mr. Caan had shown up, and he escorted us out of there. And while Heather was blubbering all over our jolly old vice principal, trying to convince him what a terrorist I was, I thanked Officer Borsch for showing up and then said, "What are you going to do with her?"

He shrugged. "Ruffle her feathers some. Introduce her

to a horse—show her how heavy they are. I don't know. I have to give it some thought." He chuckled and said, "I really didn't think I'd have the opportunity to do anything, but I'm glad I decided to come."

"What changed your mind, anyway?"

He looked away, and I realized he wasn't turning red from anger—he was blushing.

"What? What happened?"

He shrugged. "Debra overheard our conversation and accused me of being an old fart."

"Debra?" I almost blurted, You mean the Vagrant Dodo? but instead, I buttoned my lip, swirled my hand around my head, and said, "You mean the lady with the...um...the *hair*?"

He nodded, then said, "And here I thought I'd be going back with proof that this was the wackiest idea anyone had ever come up with." He said through a chuckle, "You always manage to surprise me, Samantha."

I laughed, then said, "Oh! By the way...is the guy that's been roasting you at work named Andy Hicks?"

Officer Borsch squinted at me. "How *do* you find this stuff out?"

I shrugged. "Elyssa's mom said something about it."

Officer Borsch scowled. "He's the one, all right." He hiked up his gun belt and said, "I know you probably think I have no sense of humor, but you're wrong. I've just got no sense of humor where Andy Hicks is concerned. He's a bad seed."

"Like crooked?"

He hesitated, then decided to tell me. "Jim Keltner

and I tried to prove it a few years back, but we got nowhere."

I dug out the page from Mrs. Landvogt's bible and gave it to him. "Well, Merry Christmas."

The more he read, the more bridgework he showed. Finally he whispered, "Where did you *get* this?"

"Let's just say I snatched it from the jaws of a crocodile." I smiled at him. "It's all yours. Have fun."

He just stood there blinking at me, so I laughed and said, "If you'll excuse me, I've got a gift to deliver."

Now, Santa Caan was not about to let me scoot off without an explanation. He corrals Officer Borsch and the rest of us together, and for once, I let Officer Borsch do all the talking. And when he had straightened everything out, the three of us charged off to the bathroom to get cleaned up.

When we returned to the cafeteria, it was like nothing had happened. People were laughing and dancing and sucking on candy canes, and over in the corner I spotted Rudy Folksmeir with a couple of his buddies, talking dirt.

I gave him the brown bag and said, "Merry Christmas, Rudy."

He opened it up kind of suspiciously, but all of a sudden his face broke into a giant smile. "Cool! Wow, guys, look at this!" He turned it over a couple of times and said, "Sammy, this is way cool!"

His friends put down their plastic canes of M&M's and said, "Dude, check it out!"

I laughed and said, "Glad you like it," and all of a sudden it felt like Christmas inside—warm and happy and kind of peaceful.

Then there was this little voice behind me, saying, "Sammy? Sammy, here. This is for you."

I turned around, and there, smiling at me through her bangs, was Cassie Kuo. She pushed a shiny red package into my hands and said, "Merry Christmas."

"You're my KK?"

She nodded and asked, "Aren't you going to open it?"

"Oh! Oh, sure." So I ripped off the wrapping and popped open the box, and what I pulled out of the tissue paper was a round ornament that spelled SAMMY around the top hemisphere and SAMMY upside down around the bottom hemisphere. It was glittery white and dangled from a red velvet ribbon, and the whole thing was made out of macaroni. I held it up and said, "Cassie, I can't believe this. Where did you get it? Did you *make* it?"

She nodded and practically wagged her tail. "Do you like it? Really?"

"It's amazing! I can't believe..." I looked right at her. "Where did you learn to do this?"

She looked around like she was afraid someone might hear. "Girl Scouts."

"*Girl* Scouts?"

"Yeah, yeah, I know. But it's really fun. We do crafts and go camping and hiking. Do you...do *you* like camping?" I could see hope right through that curtain of hair. Then she looked down and said, "You seem like you would."

"I...I don't know. I've never been."

"You've never *been*? Boy, you're missing out! You should come with us sometime. It is *so* much fun."

I tucked the ornament safely in the box. "Um..."

She whispered, "You wouldn't have to *join*, just talk to your mom—ask her if you can come along sometime."

My mom. Right. But I wasn't about to get into *that*, so I smiled and said, "Uh, yeah. Maybe so."

She kind of nodded over my shoulder and said, "Well, Marissa and them are waiting for you, so I'd better let you go." She smiled and said, "Merry Christmas!"

I stopped her. "Cassie?"

"Yeah?"

"I'm...I'm glad you were my KK. Thank you."

She smiled. "I'm glad, too. 'Bye!"

And it's funny. As soon as she scampered off I felt sad. Lonely. And even though I had friends waiting for me to join them, Cassie bringing up my mom made me realize that I couldn't just have fun hanging around with them when school let out.

There was something else I had to do.

TWENTY-TWO

I stared at her door for a long time. And when I did put the key in and turn the knob, it felt strange. Like I was Mrs. Graybill.

I went in and just sat on her sofa and thought. About her. About Billy McCabe. About how miserable she'd made herself, trying to make her sister feel bad.

Then I started thinking about the Crocodile and the whole Landvogt mess. How she'd treated Tina, and how Tina had turned into a blackmailer, just like her mom.

And through it all I could hear Hudson talking. Talking about forgiveness.

Then I did something I've tried for over a year *not* to do. I thought about my mother. About how she'd dumped me at Grams'. About the bad dreams I'd had and all the tears I'd cried because I'd missed her so much. About her promise to be back soon. About how, just when I was getting used to not hearing from her, there would be her voice on the line, telling me she loved me.

And I thought about how, when you got right down to it, what she'd done was desert me to become the GasAway Lady.

And as I sat there on Mrs. Graybill's couch, I started crying. First just a little, then like Elyssa had at the graveyard. And somehow I wound up with one of Mrs. Graybill's afghans wrapped around me, warm and soft, like arms comforting me.

When I was done watering her apartment, I let out a deep sigh and knew that there was only one way *not* to turn out like Mrs. Graybill, or worse, the Crocodile or Tina.

I had to forgive her. I had to find a way to forgive my mother.

So I closed my eyes and tried to remember everything. Not just the past year. Not just the bad stuff. Everything.

I remembered the swings at the park and the way she'd wave after me when she'd drop me off at school. I remembered how she used to call me Sunshine and tousle my hair. How she helped me learn the difference between little b and little d. How she'd sing rounds with me in the car. How she'd take me down to the farmers' market every Wednesday night, not to stock up on vegetables but just so we could walk around together.

And then I thought about how she'd cry herself to sleep some nights and could never explain to me why.

And when I was done soaking the carpet about *that*, I wiped off my face and got busy doing what I'd come there to do.

It was hard deciding. They were all so pretty. But in the end I picked a pastel pink and white one for Grams, a royal blue one for my mother, and one that looked like a sunrise for myself. I folded them up together, then took one last look around and whispered, "Thank you" as I closed the door.

When I got home, I locked myself in the bathroom with

paper and ribbons, and wrapped up the afghans, one by one. And as I placed them under our little tree, I got that feeling again. Warm, happy. Peaceful.

Now you may think it's kind of strange, giving gifts for Christmas that have been taken from a dead woman's apartment, but to me those afghans aren't just presents to put under the tree. They're like the fabric of life.

And if Mrs. Graybill were here, I don't think she'd chase me down and take them back. No, something tells me that Daisy Graybill—the real Daisy Graybill—would give them to me herself if she could.

Have you read
SAMMY KEYES and the CURSE of MOUSTACHE MARY
yet?

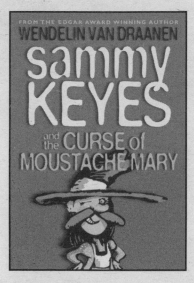

Here's a sneak peek.

PROLOGUE

You'd think I could spend the night at a friend's house without finding myself knee-deep in pig poop. But no. I couldn't even *make* it there without practically breaking every bone in my body, and by the time the clock was gonging in the New Year, well, I was in so deep it was going to take a *backhoe* to get me out.

ONE

Marissa McKenze is the last person on earth you should ever accept a ride from. And I *knew* that. Trouble is, she had a bike, Holly had a bike, and all I had were my high-tops and the distant memory of a skateboard that had disappeared while I was playing video games at the mall.

And maybe I should have wobbled around on Holly's handlebars instead, but Holly wasn't offering. Marissa was. And since Dot's new house was clear out in Sisquane and I didn't want to spend all morning getting there, what choice did I have?

Actually, things were going pretty well. Our duffel bags were in back, bungeed tight and balanced right, and it was real foggy out, so Marissa was driving kind of carefully for once. We'd made it three whole blocks down Broadway and another three whole blocks down Cook Street with-out so much as a serious wobble. But then, just as I was starting to relax a little, these guys come barreling down a cross street on skateboards.

Holly stopped. Just locked up her brakes and slid to a halt. Marissa, on the other hand, *started* to stop, but then changed her mind and decided to *go*. And as we're heading for the collision of the century, she lets go of the handlebars and cries, "Timber!"

3

She goes down sideways, and I sail through the air, straight for this guy who's ducking and weaving on his skateboard, trying to avoid me. But I'm flying at him like a human cannonball, and he doesn't have a chance. Not a prayer. I nail him, *smack!* right to the asphalt.

His skateboard goes flipping off, and his mouth does, too, letting loose with a string of four-letter synonyms for Ouch!

I untangle myself from him and hold on to my arm, because it hurts pretty bad and blood's already seeping through my sweatshirt. He's still swearing away, kind of dancing around flicking a wrist, but he interrupts himself long enough to say, "Stupid females!"

I sit there in the middle of the street holding my arm, trying to contain the pain. "I'm sorry. I...I..."

"You what?" he snaps. "You thought you could ride around town like a circus act and people would stop and cheer?"

Blood's starting to ooze through the right knee of my jeans, and since my whole body's pretty sore from having had an asphalt adjustment, I don't feel like arguing or explaining. I just sit there with my eyes closed and say, "Look, I'm sorry, okay? I'm sorry."

Then I hear someone laughing. So I look up from my private little spot in the middle of the street and what do I see? A guy with brown hair and baggy pants on his way to becoming hysterical about bruised-up bodies in the street. And I'm about to tell Baggy Boy to shut up when I hear someone *else* laughing behind me. I turn around, and there's Marissa and the guy she'd crashed into, dusting off, laughing. And then there's Holly, straddling her bike with her hand in front of her mouth, about to bust up, too.

Well. Obviously they're all just fine. And I suppose I was, too, only I wasn't ready to admit it yet. I was too mad. Mad at Marissa for being such a bad driver. Mad at my mother for buying me a pink angora sweater for Christmas instead of something I wanted—like a new skateboard or a bike. And the more I sat there, the madder I got, and the more I wanted to kill the guy who'd stolen my skateboard in the first place. I mean, if I still had it, I wouldn't be sitting there in the middle of the street all banged up from riding around town like a circus act.

Then I hear Marissa's victim say, "You don't remember me, do you?"

Marissa looks at him a little closer, then says, "Oh, yeah...you're..."

He helps her out. "Taylor. You asked me for directions the first day of school, remember?"

Well, *I* recognize him. He's Taylor Briggs, slick-and-slimy eighth grader. Good friends with Heather Acosta, red-and-rotten seventh grader. Taylor's older brother is best friends with Marissa's cousin Brandon; Taylor's the one who told Heather about Marissa being rich, and Taylor's the one who told Heather that I looked like a *fourth* grader.

Now, Heather may be cat hair in my craw, and there's probably not a kid at William Rose Junior High who doesn't know that truth to her is a foreign language—one she's not about to learn. But that first day of seventh grade, when she told me that Taylor thought I looked like a fourth grader, you could tell—there was truth behind it.

So I'm sitting there, mad at the world, mad at Marissa for laughing with a guy who's friends with Heather and thinks I look like a fourth grader, when Baggy Boy comes up to the guy I'd bombed and hands him back his skateboard. "Here you go, Snake. You all right?"

He says, "Yeah, dude. Thanks," and gives me one last glare.

I'm sitting there thinking, Snake? What kind of stupid name is Snake? when I notice the bottom of his skateboard. It's a metal-gray color, but it's been spray-painted that way. And I can tell, because underneath, where the gray's been scraped away jumping curbs, it's purple. A light purple with dark veins running through it. Like it had been dipped in molten amethyst. And there's only one other board I've ever seen that looks like that.

Mine.

I get up and say, "Hey, wait a second!"

He turns around.

"Where'd you get that skateboard?"

He sneers at me. "Oh, now you want to learn to ride? Don't *even* go there." He looks over at Baggy for a laugh. "Walkin's more your speed."

He turns to go, so I say, "No really. Wait a minute. Where'd you get it?" I run up for a better look, and when I see the foot grip, it's like my heart hits rapids.

Along the back of the foot grip, there's a three-inch strip missing. A three-inch strip completely gone except for a little piece sticking out like Florida in a States puzzle.

So between Florida on the top and amethyst on the bottom, there's no doubt in my mind: That skateboard's mine. And suddenly I'm not feeling my banged-up bones or the blood trickling down my leg. I'm feeling mad. Branding-hot mad.

I close in on the guy, saying, "Where did you *get* it?"

He's looking at me like I've got something contagious. "I bought it off a friend, okay?"

I get right in his face. "Well, where did your *friend* get it, then?"

"Hey, back off, psycho!" He looks over at Taylor, then back at me. "At a garage sale, all right? Like it's any of your business."

"It *is* my business!" I twist the board and point to the band of purple. "This is *my* skateboard and I can prove it. I wrote my initials right up here."

He snickers. "I don't see no initials."

"Scrape off the paint."

He backs away from me, so I lunge for the skateboard. "I said, scrape off the paint!"

He wrestles it out of my hands. "You *are* psycho!"

I can't just let him walk away. That's *my* skateboard. And somehow I can't find it in me to reason with the guy or have a nice little chat about how the right thing for him to do would be to give it back. No, watching him walk off with my skateboard, there's only one thing left to do.

Jump him.

I go flying through the air to tackle him again, but this time he doesn't go down. He spins and bucks and finally just throws me off. "Dude! Get a grip!"

Marissa helps me up and whispers, "It isn't worth it, Sammy. It's only a skateboard."

"But it's *my* skateboard, and he knows it!"

Holly calls, "Yeah! Hey—that thing's pretty beat-up anyway. Why don't you scrape the paint off and settle this?" She shrugs. "Unless you're lying and *you* stole it."

Snake takes a step toward us. "Who you callin' a liar? You think I'd want to *steal* this thing?"

Taylor plants himself between us like a road-wrestling referee. "He is telling the truth. He bought it off me." He shrugs. "I got it at a garage sale for five bucks."

Well, that buttons my beak. Finally I choke out, "But it's *mine*."

Taylor gives me a sad little shake of the head. "If it was, it's not anymore."

Just then a primer-gray pickup truck with wide tires and huge sideview mirrors comes rumbling down the street. And the minute Taylor sees it, he practically stomps his foot. "Oh, maaaan…"

The driver cranks down the window and calls, "Get in. Mom and Dad want you back home."

There's also a guy in the back of the pickup, and he leans out and calls to Taylor, "Hop into the paddy wagon, bro. The gestapo's out in force."

Marissa whispers, "Is that Karl?"

I whisper back, "Who's Karl?"

"Brandon's best friend, remember?"

Now maybe it was, but the guy in the back of the truck wasn't anyone I recognized as being any kind of friend of Brandon's. I mean, I'd been to pool parties at Brandon's before, and this guy sure didn't look like anyone I'd ever seen him with.

Marissa whispers, "God, that *is* Karl. His hair's gotten long, and he looks…I don't know, *older,* but that's him."

Baggy Boy goes over and asks for a ride, and pretty soon Snake's on board, too, only none of them are in the cab. They're piled up like a load of cattle in the back, settling in as Big Brother grinds into gear and lets out the clutch.

So off they go into the fog with my skateboard. And all of a sudden my body's aching and I can feel the blood crusting my jeans to my knee, and all I want is to sit down and cry.

Marissa sees the sleeve of my sweatshirt and says, "Maybe we should take you to a doctor."

"I don't need a doctor!"

Holly comes over and says, "Let me see," and makes me pull my arm out of the sleeve. Marissa about faints when she sees the scrape, but Holly turns my arm back and forth and says, "You just need some gauze and tape. A doctor can't do anything for that."

I don't happen to have a box of gauze and a roll of tape handy, and I sure didn't want to go home to dig some up. But then Marissa asks, "Do you think Hudson will have some?"

Hudson! Of course! We were only a few blocks from his house, and if anyone in Santa Martina could patch me up, it was Hudson Graham.

Not that Hudson's a doctor or anything. He's seventy-two and retired—from what, I'm not real sure—but what

I do know is that he's a friend I can count on, and he's got the tools to fix anything. Including a scraped arm and a banged-up knee.

So off we went to Cypress Street to find Hudson. And I was expecting him to be in a chair on his big porch, sipping tea like he always is, but when we turned up the walkway, no Hudson.

I tried the bell, then peeked in the living room window. No Hudson. And I'm just about to give up when a jogger in gray sweats and white Nikes appears on Hudson's walkway.

He might have been able to fool me altogether if it weren't for those bushy white eyebrows sticking out like fog lights from beneath his sweatshirt hood. And even after I knew it was Hudson, it still felt strange. Like discovering that the jacket you've been wearing all year is reversible.

I mean, Hudson drinks iced tea, reads books, and spends his days on his porch watching the world go by. Hudson does not wear sweats. Hudson does not jog. And Hudson Graham does not wear tennis shoes. He wears boots. Cowboy boots. Red ones, green ones, furry ones, ones that look like the hide of a Tyrannosaurus rex—boots.

So seeing him appear out of the fog in tennis shoes and sweats spooked me.

He pulls back his hood and ruffles his beacon of white hair. "Sammy, are you all right? You look pale." Then he notices the sleeve of my sweatshirt. "Here. Come up here and sit down."

He gets me onto his porch and parks me in a chair, then asks, "What happened?"

I glance over at Marissa, who starts fidgeting around, doing the McKenze dance. "They came out of nowhere. And they were going so fast!" She looks up at me. "I couldn't help it!"

Hudson sizes up the number of wheels on his walkway and the number of people on his porch and says, "You riding tandem again?"

I scowl and nod, and pull my arm out of my sweatshirt. After he inspects it, he whispers, "I thought you swore off," and heads for the house.

I call after him, "I did! But Dot's moved out to Sisquane, and I can't exactly *walk* that far."

A minute later Hudson's back with a first aid kit, and while he's cleaning me up, I tell him about our little crash-dummy convention and how I wouldn't have to be riding on Marissa's handlebars if my skateboard hadn't been stolen.

When I'm all done, he says, "This whole situation could also have been avoided if you'd asked me for a ride." I keep twitching away from him, because he's scrubbing pretty good and it stings. But he pins my arm down and says, "I'm surprised your grandmother didn't insist." He eyes me. "She *does* know what you're doing, doesn't she?"

"She knows I'm spending the weekend at Dot's..."

One bushy white eyebrow arches up.

"And I told her Marissa was giving me a ride..."

His eyebrow arches up even higher. "But...?"

11

I look down and confess, "But I never told her that the *ride* Marissa was giving me was on her handlebars."

He studies me with a frown, then pops open some disinfectant and smears it all over my arm. "A vital piece of information conveniently omitted?"

"I didn't *lie*. I just didn't tell her."

Hudson doesn't say a word. He just puts gauze on my arm, wraps it up, and starts working on my knee. And I'm feeling bad, like I *did* lie. "Hudson, it was either go with Grams to visit Lady Lana or spend New Year's at Dot's. What would *you* have done?"

"Rita's gone to Hollywood?"

"Uh-huh. And she was really pushing for me to go with her." I scowl at him and mutter, "Like I want to start my New Year with a tour of the set they used for Lady Lana's GasAway commercial."

"Could've been interesting to see your mother's work environment."

"It would've been torture! Besides, seeing her for two days at Christmas was enough to last me for another year."

Hudson sighs and says, "I heard about your angora sweater."

"It's *pink*."

"I know." He tries to stifle a grin. "I guess I'd have chosen Dot's, too."

"Exactly."

Hudson snaps his first aid kit closed. "So let's get you there in one piece, shall we? I'd give you a ride, but I sense that being chauffeured is not what you had in mind."

"It's really nice of you, but I..."

"But you don't want a lift when your friends are riding."

I shrug. "Yeah."

Marissa and Holly have been kind of standing around, keeping quiet, but when Marissa hears that, she says, "Maybe our bikes would fit in the trunk?"

Hudson smiles. "I have a better idea."

He disappears down the side steps, and when he comes back, about ten minutes later, he's pushing a bike alongside him. Now this bike is old, but it's old like his car, Jester. Shiny old. Tons-of-chrome old. Whitewall-tires old. Way-too-cool-to-ride old.

I take one look at it and say, "You're kidding, right?"

"Not at all. What am I saving it for? It's just collecting dust."

"But what if I wreck it?"

He throws his head back and laughs. "Then you wreck it. It's seen a few adventures in its lifetime. A few more won't hurt."

So we divvied up the duffels and started off again, and let me tell you, I couldn't stop smiling. Hudson's bike was smooth and fast, and the wind in my face felt like something I hadn't known in ages. It felt like freedom.

But if I'd had any idea what we were riding toward, I'd have turned right around, returned the bike, and jumped the next train to Hollywood.

Don't miss these other great books by Wendelin Van Draanen:

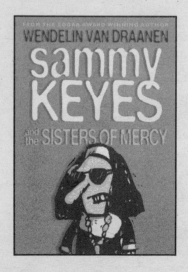

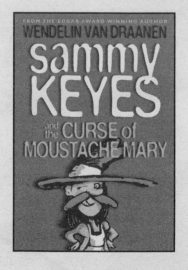

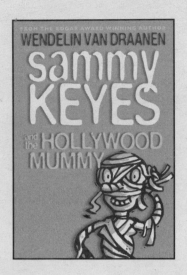

FROM THE EDGAR AWARD WINNING AUTHOR
WENDELIN VAN DRAANEN
sammy
KEYES
and the HOLLYWOOD MUMMY

FROM THE EDGAR AWARD WINNING AUTHOR
WENDELIN VAN DRAANEN
sammy
KEYES
and the SEARCH for SNAKE EYES

FROM THE EDGAR AWARD WINNING AUTHOR
WENDELIN VAN DRAANEN
sammy
KEYES
and the ART of DECEPTION

WENDELIN VAN DRAANEN

FLIPPED

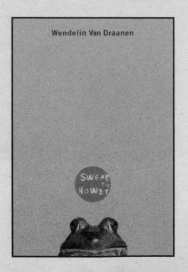

Wendelin Van Draanen

SWEAR TO HOWDY